PINKY PROMISE

Elle M Thomas

Cover design and editing by Bookfully Yours
Formatting by Lia V Dias

This is an Elle M Thomas mature, contemporary romance.
Anyone who has read my work before will know what that
means, but if you're new to me then let me explain.
This book includes adult situations including, but not
limited to adult characters that swear, a lot. A leading man
who talks dirty, really, really dirty. Sex, lots and lots of hot,
steamy, sheet gripping and toe-curling sex. Due to the dark
and explicit nature of this book, it is recommended for
mature audiences only.
If this is not what you want to read about then this might
not be the book for you, but if it is then sit back, buckle up
and enjoy the ride.

Other titles by Elle M Thomas:

Disaster-in-Waiting
Revealing His Prize
One Night Or Forever

Love in Vegas Series (to be read in order)
Lucky Seven (Book 1)
Pushing His Luck (Book 2)
Lucking Out (Book 3)

Falling Series (to be read in order)
New Beginnings (Book 1)
Still Falling (Book 2)

The Nanny Chronicles (to be read in order)
Single Dad (Gabe and Carrie)
Pinky Promise (Seb and Bea)

Dedication

To overcoming fears and chasing dreams

Chapter One

Seb

"So, what's the plan?"

I looked across at my oldest friend, Gabe, who really did look like the cat who'd got the cream and swallowed a canary. He kind of had. He had gone from being single, widowed, with a little girl of three-years-old and then he'd hired a nanny. A nanny he hadn't wanted but had fancied the pants off, literally, and after a few bumps in the road they'd got their acts together. I did take some credit for that.

"The plan is as I told you it was last night; breakfast, shower, get dressed and marry my angel." Gabe smiled, confidence oozing from him, knowing this was the first day of the rest of his life with his perfect woman.

I wondered what that felt like, having been hurt in the past, burnt by trusting and loving, only to find the strength to try again, to trust, and to love again.

My friend stared at me as I tried to temper my own thoughts and emotions.

"You all good?" he asked with a slightly concerned frown.

"Yeah, why wouldn't I be?" I heard the snap in my voice but was incapable of stopping it.

"If that doesn't tell me you're not, I don't know what does."

"Fuck off, Gabe."

He laughed at me and then shook his head. "Me and you are going for breakfast and we are going to talk this through, whether you want to or not because today is my wedding day. It is going to be perfect, Carrie and Charlotte deserve for it to be perfect, so the fact that we both know that it's your past relationship with the bridesmaid that's eating you, it needs resolving."

"We didn't have a relationship. We fucked, no more." I was being a dick because I was agitated and becoming more pissed off with every second that passed. I knew that every second that passed was taking me ever closer to coming face to face with Bea.

"Then there won't be a problem, will there, if you only fucked her? We both know there have been dozens, if not hundreds of women you have fucked. Women you only ever viewed as convenient and willing, and you've never had an issue with them, so Bea won't be any different, will she?"

"Fuck off, Gabe." I couldn't bring myself to say that maybe, just maybe, this was a little different.

Because it wasn't.

He laughed at me, like he could almost hear my internal monologue, and turned to pick up his wallet, phone and room key. "You need some new lines, buddy."

"Fuck you, you smug, arrogant fucker."

With a small shake of his head, he grinned.

"If today wasn't your wedding day, I would spread your nose across your face."

"Yeah, like you're man enough to do that."

I flipped him off and he shrugged it off with a smile. The truth was, I wasn't much of a fighter, I was the typically laid back one of the two of us. Gabe was the fiery one, always had been, and was the one who threw the punches. I was more likely to get punched by an angry boyfriend or husband due to the lack of relationship status I had, there wasn't a tick box for womaniser. I liked being with a woman for a good time then walking away, sometimes asking about their relationship status got lost in translation.

My mind went back to the night we'd found a guy, Toby, attempting to rape Carrie after drugging her. The sight of her being touched by him whilst clearly stoned almost to the point of unconsciousness will haunt me forever, so I could only imagine how that played on my friend's mind. He had been frantic as we tried to find her then relieved when we had. His relief was short lived. In the second he saw her, saw Toby touching her, something went off in his head and the short fuse he had been working with burnt out completely.

Gabe had grabbed for the other man who was slightly taken aback to have been discovered, so probably didn't see the first blow coming, but all the others that followed, well, he felt every one of those, even if he hadn't seen them all. Gabe rained blow after blow on him, while I took care of Nanny, trying to get her to come around a little as I covered her up. I was also the one to call the police as my friend continued his attack on Toby.

As much as I understood Gabe's need to pummel him—and why wouldn't I? —truth be told I would have happily punched the fucker myself for what he'd done to Nanny. However, I also needed my friend not to end up being arrested and charged with a serious assault or murder! So, with reasonable force still arguable, I pulled my friend clear and redirected his attention to his woman.

I allowed myself a small, ironic, internal chuckle as I recalled that fucking animal attempting to get up and possibly make a run for it. I'd even threatened him with a punch of my own at that point, and truth be told, I think I would have enjoyed it. Thank fuck he was locked up for a minimum of ten years, although in a psychiatric unit rather than prison. I briefly wondered what would happen to him if he was deemed of sound mind before the ten years. Would he be transferred to a prison to serve the remainder of that time? I had no clue and now was not the time to discuss this with my friend, this was his wedding day. This was Nanny's day. I was even more determined than ever to ensure they both, but especially Nanny, got the day she wanted and deserved. There was something truly special about her. She was funny, kind, and took no shit, not really, but there was more than that for me. I loved how she loved Gabe, but by far her most redeeming quality for me was the way she loved Charlotte. I loved that kid as much as if she was my own, and so did Nanny. That little girl had been through far more than she knew, although one day she would know and would need to be loved by everyone in her life, even more than she did now, and to be happy, and Carrie, well she did that in the most magnificent way and I trusted her to always do that.

Now, I was the one thinking that his bride deserved the perfect day but was still pissed off, with what, or who, I wasn't fully prepared to admit yet, not even to myself and as my friend was the only one here, well, all of my angst would be heading his way. Even as I thought that I felt bad, but I couldn't magic up a stranger or someone I didn't care about to turn my mood on. Plus, even if I could, would I? Probably not because I wasn't an arsehole, generally, and my moods were private. I only really revealed them, the negative ones to those I trusted, so basically Gabe. Yeah, he was going to have to deal with my bad mood and anger.

"I mean it, if it wasn't for the fact that I love Nanny, and it would make her sad that I'd punched you on a day where photos would haunt you for the rest of your natural life, you'd be nursing a broken nose. Although, if I did it, she might see that I was always the better looking one and she'd come away with me."

He shot me a glare that said I was getting to him. Thinking, or suggesting that I might be thinking of Nanny in naked terms always riled him. I was a man, and she was one hot nanny.

"I reckon Nanny and I would make a very attractive couple, sexy, really, really sexy."

"Seb," he warned in his firm tone.

I laughed. I was being a dick to him, and he didn't deserve it. "Fuck, you're too easy to wind up. Come on, let's get the condemned man a hearty breakfast and I promise to be on my best behaviour, unless Bea rocks up with a new guy and then all bets are off." I was deadly serious, and that was going to be a real issue.

"For fuck's sake. I have no clue if she's bringing anyone. However, I doubt she is as she only dumped your arse four months ago."

Long-term, serious relationships were not my thing. We'd agreed in advance that we were both looking for fun, no expectations and no commitments beyond us being exclusive, which was a big thing for me. We didn't even have an argument. At the very beginning we discussed things, and both said that if either of us decided we were done, we'd say. We'd promised, pinky promised, no less. She'd called time on things when I thought everything was going well. It had bruised my ego as I was usually the one to end things, but not this time, not with Princess Bea. It wasn't even the fact that she'd ended things with *me*, it was the fact that it had ended *full stop*.

"Seb, come on. I need food."

Like a sulky teenager, I followed my friend out, shuffling my feet and huffing as I went, incapable of thinking of anything other than Bea now and whether she had brought a plus one with her.

****

Gabe was pacing the room, waiting for me to finish getting ready.

"I will go without you," he threatened.

"I am fastening my shoes and then I need to figure out how this fucking tie works."

"It's a cravat, and it fastens with a pin."

I stood up, having fastened my shoes and laughed at my friend. "Well, sorry for not knowing that, Gok Wan."

We both laughed but I was more than grateful that he knew how to fasten the bloody cravat. Who the hell wore one of these anyway?

"Isn't a cravat what posh people put wine into?" I asked.

Gabe smacked my shoulder. "That's a carafe, you bell end."

"I knew that," I protested, making my friend arch a brow disbelievingly. "Now, today is all about you and Nanny and my beautiful girl, Charlotte, so let's go and find your girls."

We exchanged matching grins. He was more than ready to find them both and nobody deserved happiness more than him and his girls.

With our jackets on, we were good to go.

"Seb," he called to me as he reached the door.

He sounded serious, so I gave him my undivided attention.

"I text Carrie earlier. Bea has come alone, no new guy."

"Thank you." I was unsure when I'd last felt that relieved. If

I'd ever felt that relieved about a woman before.

Chapter Two

Bea

Watching Carrie having her hair and make-up done was interesting. She was totally at ease, completely relaxed and it was quite clear that she didn't have a single doubt in her mind about what she was doing.

Marrying Gabe was the thing she wanted to do most in the world. She'd said that to me on her hen night a couple of weeks before. I'd believed her but seeing was very believing.

Sitting next to her was Charlotte. She was Gabe's daughter and the most delightful four-year-old I might ever have met. Seb adored her and I could understand why. I shook my head, as if by doing that I could shake him from my mind. No chance. I couldn't stop thinking about him at the best of times and today that was going into overdrive. Today was about love and happy ever afters. How the hell was I meant to forget about the man who made my heart dance to its own beat? Or more, his beat. When I'd ended things between us it was for the best, or at least that's what I'd told myself, but as each day and every lonelier night passed, I was questioning it more and more. Today was going to be incredibly difficult.

Charlotte's laughter, at something I'd missed, made me refocus my attention on the little girl before me. She was pretty, funny, and desperate for Carrie to really be her mummy.

They each wore identical robes with their title on the back. I had one too. Mine had chief bridesmaid on. Gabe's mum had mother of the groom on hers. I liked her, mainly because she loved Carrie and encouraged her relationship with her son. Carrie's robe said bride and Charlotte's said daughter of the bride. When we'd all been given them last night, Charlotte had cried, then Carrie had cried, we all cried, even Gabe who had been there via Facetime.

Charlotte's hair was going up in a bun, a slightly tighter and tidier bun than Carrie, who was having the finishing touches to her loose, but secure up do added. She had some loose strands curled before a jewelled headband was put in place. The band was embellished with glittery, sparkly stones and sat around her head like a crown almost and then she had a veil that matched perfectly.

"Ta-da," said the stylist once Carrie was complete.

Her make-up had been done in a very natural and understated way and she still looked like Carrie. Charlotte had looked distraught when she'd been told that she didn't need make-up, so the make-up artist had added a little colour to her cheeks, eyes and lips. Carrie's fingers and toes had been treated to some treatments a few days before including glittery French polishes, and not surprisingly, Charlotte's fingernails were currently matching. That little girl adored Carrie and loved anything they had the same.

"You look beautiful," cried Christine, Gabe's mum, with tears in her eyes. "Gabe will be beyond happy."

Carrie grinned. "Well, as that was the plan, I've succeeded."

"What about me, Grandma?" Charlotte squealed with excitement as her sparkly band, that had the same design as Carrie's, was fitted around her bun.

"You might be even more beautiful than you usually are," her grandmother told her.

The little girl giggled. "Then we are all beautiful. You, Bea, me and Carrie, oh and Daddy and Uncle Seb, they are beautiful too."

"They certainly are," Carrie agreed, leaning down to kiss the little girl's nose.

"And Grandad and Granny." She giggled as she uttered the word Granny, but then from all I knew of Gabe's grandmother, her and her inappropriateness that I wasn't convinced was entirely down to her dementia, made most people laugh.

I fought a little giggle myself before Carrie started to move things along. "Right then, Potty Lottie, you need to go with Grandma to get your dress on and Bea and I will go and put ours on too."

"Yes!"

I laughed at the little girl who had woke up on the hour every hour from two that morning, asking if she could put her dress on.

"I am so happy for you," I told Carrie as I zipped her into her dress.

"Thank you. I had no idea that this level of happy existed."

I smiled at her, but even I knew it was lacking and a little forced.

"Are you okay, with seeing Seb?" she asked, and I hid my sigh at her knowing me too well.

I shrugged. I had no idea how I was about seeing him.

"Bea, talk to me. I still don't understand what happened?"

I sniffed loudly. "Is he here with someone? Has he got someone new?" I wasn't sure that was the appropriate response to my friend's questions, but it was where I was at. He really did crowd my every waking thought.

Carrie smiled, then let out a small laugh. "You two need your heads banging together. Gabe messaged me last night to ask if you had a plus one because Seb was going mad thinking that you might not be alone."

I could have kicked myself, but the smile breaking across my face was going nowhere. "Really? Maybe I should have brought someone gorgeous along then."

Carrie shook her head and this time was not laughing. "You two need punching, never mind your heads banging together."

"Sorry." My smile broadened into a grin and we both laughed.

"You are so not sorry. Listen, twenty minutes before I get married is not the ideal time to discuss what happened and your current devious ways of making Seb jealous, but when I come back off my honeymoon, we should talk, properly. You can tell me what happened and what you want, okay."

"Yes, thank you. And in case I haven't mentioned this, those tiny and very expensive lacy scraps you're wearing beneath your dress won't last a minute once your man gets you alone."

Carrie actually blushed at that and then, with a coy little smile replied. "Then they'll be worth every bloody penny."

"I am so glad we met and became friends."

"Me too, otherwise I'd have had no chief bridesmaid."

I made as if to punch her in the arm but pulled her in for a hug. "Right then, let's get you married and give Charlotte a real mummy."

Chapter Three

Seb

The wedding was to be an intimate affair. The guests were few in number, but plentiful in love and best wishes for the bride and groom. Carrie had no family as such, just a couple of distant aunts and cousins from her adoptive parents, both of whom were dead. Her natural family were also dead, well, her mother, and she knew of no others. I had often wondered how she had managed not to be bitter about that when she saw the love and closeness of other people's families, although she was now a part of our family, so she had it all.

I looked across at Gabe before we entered the drawing room in this country hotel where the wedding was taking place. It had high walls with ornamental mouldings around the edge of the room and the ceiling, giving it a classic feel, and whilst luxurious it was in no way ostentatious. Even the large chandeliers that hung in a row down the centre of the room screamed good taste. I was no expert in interior design but the way they'd stuck to the blank canvas of cream ensured that regardless of the bridal party's colour scheme, it wouldn't cause an issue. The registrar was positioned in a huge bay window that looked out onto the lush, green grounds and beyond, a clear, blue sky greeted us as the sun shined down on my wonderful friends who would stand before her, basking in the sun's warmth and light. The window offered a picture-perfect frame for the three of them to stand within.

"You okay?"

Gabe was showing the first hint of nerves as he shifted from one foot to the other, then took a deep breath, preparing to enter the room. I removed my hand from the door handle.

"Yeah. I just want it to be perfect for her."

I smiled. He wasn't even nervous for himself, but for Carrie. He wouldn't have given a shit if they'd got married in jeans and t-shirts during a wet Wednesday lunch break, but this, he was giving Carrie the wedding she wanted and deserved.

"It will be." I slapped his back. "She wants to marry you and have Charlotte as her own and that will happen today, so, it will be perfect."

He smiled.

"I mean anyone in their right mind would want my beautiful Charlotte in their life, but you..."

He jabbed his finger in my arm but pulled me in for a hug.

"Is this a gay wedding? I had a lovely gay friend. Lovely hands, and he had legs to die for."

Gabe and I laughed as Margaret, his grandmother who'd just arrived, misunderstood our man hug. She hadn't ever had much of a filter, but now, with dementia, there was nothing she wouldn't and didn't say.

Gabe turned to her, Gabe who she often mistook for his grandfather who he was a dead ringer for. "Here's my sexy little minx. And don't you look even more gorgeous than ever."

Gabe's mother rolled her eyes while his father looked concerned that she was about to go off on one.

"Christopher, lover," she cooed.

"Shit," muttered Noel, Gabe's dad.

"Are you gay now? Are you having a gay wedding?"

She looked at me and smiled as she ran a lingering glance across me.

"Although, I'd be more than happy to give him a test drive."

I laughed and couldn't resist giving her a wink which made her blush. This was the sort of woman every man needed to grow old with.

"I was something of a ground breaker," she told me. "Always open to suggestion. Has Christopher told you about our times in Paris?"

I swore Christine and Noel were ready to vomit or have a stroke at her revelations.

Gabe interrupted. "Temptress, Paris was all ours, ssh." He leaned in and gave her a peck on the cheek. "Now, go and find your seat, and remember, best behaviour."

With his family members going through to join the congregation, we both laughed.

"Good luck with perfect."

We both sniggered like naughty schoolboys. Gabe pulled his phone out and began to type. I leaned across and was in no way surprised that he was texting Carrie.

<Miss Webber, I am waiting for you, I need to see you, Angel x>

"I'll miss Carrie fucking Webber," I said, thinking of how he used to call her that when she was getting under his skin.

He smiled, clearly remembering Carrie fucking Webber.

"But now she will be Carrie fucking Caldwell."

I smirked, considered his words and was unable to resist one poke of the bear. "Yeah and you will be fucking Carrie Caldwell."

He frowned and opened his mouth, ready to rebuke me, but his phone bleeped, distracting him.

<Mr Caldwell, I am on my way and cannot wait to see you x>

"Let's go." My friend confidently grinned and we entered the room and took our places at the front.

Gabe was excited and happier than I'd ever seen him, even when I'd been his best man for his first wedding. Me, on the other hand; I was hot and cold, felt sick, nervous, my stomach rolled and churned, and I was sure I was sweating. Thank fuck it wasn't me getting married, especially if this was the state I was in as best man. I coughed, hoping to move the huge lump I could feel there and admitted, if only to myself that I was not nervous about being Gabe's best man. I was not worried about standing up and making a speech, it was hilarious and guaranteed to be loved by all. The reason for my impending breakdown or whatever the fuck this was, was all down to seeing Princess Bea again. I needed to stay calm, get a grip and not humiliate myself by following her around like a lovesick puppy. No, I needed to put my game face on and find a distraction.

Bea? Bea who?

Music started and looking back we saw that the doors were open.

Showtime.

Chapter Four

Bea

We had just got ourselves sorted and descended the stairs. Carrie had a small bag that was no more than a fabric, drawstring pouch that glittered and glimmered. Christine was supposed to take it with her but as she was going to rescue Noel from Margaret, she'd forgotten it, so Carrie was now carrying it with her flowers.

Her phone sounded from inside the bag making us all laugh.

She pulled it out, grinned soppily at a message from Gabe and immediately replied, then flicked her screen in my direction. For the final time he had called her Miss Webber and she had addressed him as Mr Caldwell.

I smiled at her and the love they shared as she put it on silent, put it away and passed the bag to Charlotte.

"Can you look after this for me?"

The little girl nodded, and Carrie secured the bag, that also contained her engagement ring, around her wrist.

"So, you have my bag and when I am marrying Daddy, Bea will hold my flowers. Right then, my girls, let's do this getting married thing!"

I laughed, watching on as Carrie strode away, virtually running as she got nearer to the closed door that stood between her and her groom.

Carrie had no family of her own, not really, so she had nobody to give her away. She had briefly considered asking her future father-in-law but opted against that. She had finally decided that she didn't need to be given away. She belonged to nobody other than Gabe and as such she would give herself over for a final time at the altar.

I allowed myself a smile when I recalled Seb volunteering to do the job. He had gone on and on about Nanny, which is what he called Carrie, being his and how he might have to seriously consider giving her to Gabe. Gabe had laughed initially, but soon tired of his best friend insisting that as he'd singlehandedly got them back together, he had won the right to have Nanny belong to him. The two of them had a wonderful relationship. They really were the best of friends. Lifelong friends and now Carrie was firmly entrenched within that tight circle. Briefly, I wondered if I would eventually be pushed out of the foursome we had, especially now that Seb and I were no longer a couple, more so because I had ended things. I didn't doubt that if it came down to a straight choice between the two of us, Gabe would have no doubts in choosing Seb. That left Carrie, and as much as we'd grown close quickly, her priority would be her husband and family, of which my former beau was an intrinsic member.

"Do I go in first?" asked Charlotte, bringing me back into things and organising us all.

There was a woman from the venue there. She nodded and Charlotte turned to face the front.

"Then you," she turned her attention to me. "Are you okay, lovely?" She looked quite concerned.

I felt many things, but none of them felt like okay. My head was spinning, my stomach was turning over, and I felt shivery, but rather hot and clammy at the same time. My legs felt weak, as if they might just buckle beneath me and at that point I wasn't sure whether I was going to be sick or have the type of accident I hadn't had since I was about four-years-old and in nursery.

The kind woman was beginning to offer me water, or maybe a seat.

Carrie gently pushed her aside and looked me in the eyes. "Babe," she started with a gentle, calm tone. "If you are actually unwell we can get you sat down and sorted, however, if this is down to your ridiculous decision to ditch the best man four months ago, you need to pull yourself together and suck it up."

The nice lady looked on aghast.

Carrie didn't notice it, or at least chose not to as she continued. "The most wonderful man is waiting about thirty feet away for me, to marry me. I am going to be his wife and Charlotte's mummy. My fiancé is the most wonderful of men and he deserves this to be perfect and for it to go smoothly. Charlotte needs it to go off without a hitch. I need this to run exactly as we planned because this, me and Gabe and our family, is the best thing I've ever been involved in."

I nodded, loving how much her need for perfection was down to Gabe and Charlotte rather than herself.

"So, are you ill or rethinking..." she covered Charlotte's ears. "...the stupid decision to ditch Seb because you were shitting yourself when you realised you were falling hard for him, no matter how much of a fucking dickhead or man whore he is?"

I stared at her, as did the poor woman watching us.

"And that is not me bad mouthing him. God help me, I love the fucking dickhead, man whore that he is."

I couldn't help but laugh, but it totally centred me and allowed me to refocus on fulfilling my chief bridesmaid's responsibilities.

With a determined nod, I was good to go. Carrie removed her hands from Charlotte's ears, and I took my position behind the little girl who turned and looked at us before stunning the nice lady again when she innocently asked my friend, "What's a man whore?"

Carrie and I laughed loudly and fortunately my friend answered. "Uncle Seb, but they're bad words to use, so we shouldn't say them again, okay?"

The little girl nodded with a smile.

"Right, let's get this wedding on the road." Carrie took her position behind me and then looking at Charlotte, asked, "Are you ready to become my very own little girl then, Loopy Lottie?"

The little girl's eyes filled with happy tears as mine filled with pure emotion. Charlotte nodded at her soon-to-be stepmother. "Are you ready to be my mummy, Carrie?"

Carrie wafted her hand in front of her face, desperate not to cry and spoil her make-up before Gabe saw her. "Charlotte, baby, I am so, so ready. I cannot wait to be your mummy. I am so excited to marry Daddy, but I am just as excited to be your mummy, forever."

The nice lady began to sniff as tears appeared to be filling her eyes, making us all laugh and suck back our own tears once more.

"Now, let's get married," Carrie said, and the lady opened the doors.

Chapter Five

Seb

Tears pricked my eyes at the sight of Charlotte travelling down the aisle first. Gabe and I exchanged a tear-filled glance at the sight of our little girl looking every inch the princess. The kid was beaming so much she looked as though she might burst with the love she held for her dad, but also for Carrie, her soon to be mummy. If anyone deserved to have a mummy who adored them it was that little girl. Briefly, I wondered how and when she'd be told the details of her natural mother and just how my precious girl would cope and process that. She would have me and her father, both of whom had the professional ability to help her do that as well as our unconditional love, but she'd have Carrie too, someone who had chosen to love her rather than loving her by circumstance.

Charlotte came to a standstill at the front and stepped to the side, opposite us. She looked back along the aisle and both Gabe and I followed her eyes.

"Fuck." Fortunately, I managed to whisper the single word as I set eyes on Bea, walking down the aisle towards me. I needed to quash thoughts of her, an aisle and walking towards me. That had never been a possibility, not really, and now it was a definite impossibility.

Gabe looked at me over his shoulder and laughed a single, short laugh. "Yup."

I diverted my glance back to the beautiful woman heading towards me. Bea was not my usual type. I liked beautiful women, but before Bea I went for obvious beauty and attributes; tall, leggy, chesty, false eyelashes and nails, everything a little over the top and in your face. I didn't consider any of those things bad, but somehow it made me feel safe, as if with all those things hiding the real them, it meant I could hide the real me. Bea was natural; she had long, dark blonde hair, bluey-grey eyes, her nails were short and painted in a pale pink or neutral shade. Her make-up was minimal, and light and her clothes were well fitted but begged you to imagine what was beneath them rather than handing it to you on a plate.

And then I went to a bar with Gabe where Carrie happened to be with her friend, Princess Bea and with our friends dancing and making eyes at each other, we'd chatted and laughed, and got on like a house on fire. From that first second, there'd been a connection. We fancied each other, but we'd also liked each other as people. The banter was easy and off the scale. Neither of us had wanted serious, we'd agreed that on the first night, shook on it, with a pinky promise. We'd pinky promised on many things after that and it became our thing. It meant that we weren't playing games or messing the other around.

I'd taken her home that first night and we'd spent the night together. The sex was phenomenal and not in a wild, swing from the chandelier kind of way. I'd had my fair share of wild sex and this had been so much better and had continued to improve each time we did it. Everything was great, or so I thought, and then, four months later, it wasn't.

With a deep breath and a push back of my shoulders, I stood straighter, taller, stronger. I nodded at the vision in gold, an acknowledgement of her presence as she took her place next to Charlotte. She smiled and I immediately returned it, only to realise that her smile had been for Gabe, not me. So now I felt like a needy prick, returning the smile of the girl who'd dumped me after she'd smiled at someone else. Knowing that my angst was rising and unsure how to temper it, I looked away, to the open door that was now filled with the vision in white lace that was Carrie.

"Oh, Nanny."

The words fell from my mouth of their own accord and once

out I had expected a withering glance from the groom who stood just in front of me. There wasn't one. His gaze was fixed on his beautiful bride who walked down the aisle alone. He did, however, give me a rather sharp elbow to the ribs. A few members of the congregation laughed, including Bea who looked at me again and with a smile curling her delicious lips she gave me a little shake of her head.

I smiled and then looked back to Carrie who was travelling down the aisle and radiating warmth, love and hope.

She came to a standstill before Gabe and passed her flowers to Bea. Then, with her hands empty she reached up and cupped his face. "Mr Caldwell."

His grin virtually split his face open. "And for the final time, Miss Webber."

She laughed and then blushed, looking more adorable than ever.

"I quite like that nobody is giving you to me," he told her, referring to her solo trip down the aisle.

"I don't belong to anyone other than you, so…"

It was like nothing and nobody else existed for them. They were oblivious. Gabe moved into her touch and leaned in to kiss her lips gently. The registrar coughed loudly while the congregation laughed.

"We haven't got to that bit yet," the registrar said to more laughter.

Gabe straightened and shrugged while Carrie blushed a little more.

Everyone refocused and were all ready for the service to begin when a single voice spoke, Margaret. "If this is the wedding, the honeymoon won't be going off with anything other than a bang."

People muttered and sniggered while Gabe leaned in towards Carrie. "The minx has spoken, Angel."

Chapter Six

Bea

The wedding was relatively short, but beautiful in every way. Gabe and Carrie had written their own vows that were intimate, personal, and brought tears to many eyes. I tried to remain focused on Charlotte and the happy couple. I managed that for the most part, but there were times when all I could do was look across at Seb and stare at his handsome face and features. He was fucking gorgeous, and I missed him, terribly and not just the sex, although I missed that, too. What that man couldn't do with appendages wasn't worth knowing. My internal use of the word appendages amused me, so much so that a tiny giggle escaped me. Nobody seemed to notice, nobody except Seb who I found watching me, a half smirk on his face and his eyebrow quirked questioningly.

Just that one look had my breath hitching and everything below the waist clenching. Being this close to him was proving more difficult than I had imagined and all we had exchanged were fleeting glances.

With the words, 'I pronounce you' uttered, Gabe was already leaning in, pulling Carrie to him and kissing her.

"They'll be banging like a barn door in a storm if we stay here much longer."

I did nothing to hide my laughter at Margaret's observation, neither did Seb. He looked across and shook his head at me while Carrie and Gabe giggled, but it did break their kiss.

"I present to you, Mr and Mrs Caldwell," announced the

registrar.

There was loud applause from everyone except Charlotte who ran towards the bride and groom, hugging them both.

She looked up at them and Gabe scooped her up in his arms where she looked across at Carrie, "Hello, Mummy."

Carrie's lip and chin began to wobble before she brushed away her tears and allowed the biggest smile to spread across her face before she hugged the little girl and kissed her. "Hello, daughter," she said as Charlotte leapt across into her arms.

Everyone was moved by the private family moment we were privileged enough to be sharing, me included. I hadn't imagined how private such a public occasion could be. This wasn't just the joining of a couple, this was the making of a family and it was beautifully touching in its innocence and simplicity. I had never imagined a family of my own beyond assuming that one day I would have a husband and children, but that was as far as my plan had been formed. Until now. Until Seb.

****

When the formalities ended, Carrie and Gabe led the procession out towards the banqueting hall where the reception was due to take place.

Charlotte was walking with them, leaving me to walk behind them, with Seb. We looked at each other a little awkwardly.

"Shall we?" he asked with his bent arm held out for me.

I hesitated, unsure what to do.

He looked down at me, hurt, dejected, possibly even rejected, but that was not the reason for my hesitation. I was scared. Scared to touch or be touched by him. When I'd ended things, I had retreated. I couldn't continue to see him and hear his voice or be privy to the details of him getting on with his life, moving on with someone else. I had kept in close touch with Carrie and we saw each other several times a week, but she had respected my need to be kept out of the loop where Seb was concerned.

Now, here I was, preparing to slip my arm through his, and on one hand there was nothing that would make me happier, but on the other hand, I was petrified that once I had touched him again, spoken to him, been touched by him, I'd want that back in my life. I'd want him back in my life and that couldn't happen because if it did, he would break me beyond repair.

With a deep breath, I slipped my hand through his arm and offered a small smile. He smiled back, relief clouding his features that I had accepted his offer, eventually. The sensation of the feel of him touching me was better than I had anticipated. My skin prickled from head to toe until my whole body had come to life; every hair stood on end and goosebumps covered me. I shivered, or was it a shudder? Whatever it was, it caused my breath to hitch, my pulse rate to increase and a flush to colour my skin. I was hot and tense and was becoming aware of a dull ache, low down in my body, pulsating in my sex.

Touching Seb, fully clothed and in a public location had caused this reaction. I dreaded to think what might happen if there was any more than arm and hand contact between us.

As we passed Christine, she smiled across at us and winked at me, making me laugh.

"Well, if that isn't the best sound in the world," said Seb, tapping my fingers.

"What?" I stammered that one word. It seemed I was now incapable of speaking coherently. His effect on me was never-ending.

"Your laugh. It was always one of my favourite things about you."

I stared up at him, unsure what to say in response. One compliment had me flustered and speechless.

"Maybe I should remind you of all of my favourite things about you."

The pulsing ache of desire I'd felt earlier was even more apparent, as was the dampness there.

We had just entered the banqueting hall where we were greeted by the bride and groom, and Charlotte, of course.

Carrie pulled me in for a hug that allowed her to whisper to me. "How you doing?"

I pulled back and before I spoke, a waiter carrying champagne filled flutes passed by. I reached in and grabbed two glasses. The first I downed in one and then sipped the second before turning back to my friend and said, seriously, "This is how I'm doing."

She frowned, but by then Seb had joined us. "Nanny, you are looking as delectable as ever."

Carrie laughed at him and then, with more guests waiting to congratulate the new Mr and Mrs Caldwell, Seb put his hand on my hip, scorching me with his touch as he ushered me away.

I was going to need more champagne. Lots and lots of it.

Chapter Seven

Seb

The relatively short time it took for me to make my way to the banqueting hall with Bea on my arm had been amazing. For the first time in the four months since she'd kicked me to the curb, I felt alive, truly alive. The feel of her touching me felt as natural as anything I had ever known.

That had been several hours ago. The wedding reception was in full swing. Meals had been eaten, speeches and toasts made. There was a disco in full flow and the bride and bridesmaids were making the most of it. Gabe and Carrie had danced their first dance to some pop song that was apparently one from their playlist. Everyone had watched them dancing and then been invited to join them. It had been my plan to grab Bea and secure her undivided attention, not to mention to hold her in my arms again, if only for the duration of a song, with no plan beyond that in mind. I was beaten to Bea by some bloke who I have never seen before. I was seething as I watched him pull her into his hold. His hands fell to her hips. God, how I remembered those hips. Every single one of her curves had been consigned to memory. I relived every single inch of her skin warming and coming to life beneath my touch a dozen times a day or more. I relived, breathed and slept my time with her. God help me, I even dreamed of her soft and delectable body, of her. And now, seeing her in someone else's hold infuriated me. Bastard. I was all but ready to storm over and demand he unhand her, but then there was a tug on my sleeve.

"Uncle Seb, can I dance with you, please?"

When I looked down and saw my girl was without a dance partner I knew any plans to dance with Bea would have to wait a while. I picked Charlotte up and together we worked the dancefloor, bypassing the bride and groom several times.

On each occasion, Charlotte called to them, "Mummy, Daddy."

I dunno about them, but I had a huge ball of emotion clogging my throat every time she said it. She had everything she had ever wanted, and it was no more than she deserved. A small, nagging voice in my head began to ask me what it was I wanted and whether I deserved it. The song ended and a faster, dance track came on. I put Charlotte on her feet, and she was quickly whisked away by Carrie who along with Bea took centre stage to dance, which is where they still were.

"Let me get you a drink, you look like you need it." Gabe put an arm around my shoulders and led me to a quiet corner, close enough to still see the girls, but far enough away that we had some privacy. "I'd ask if you were okay, but I have eyes."

He handed me a large measure of scotch whilst taking a smaller one for himself.

"This is hard."

Gabe nodded, with genuine understanding. "Might be the hardest thing you ever do, especially if you don't put it right."

"How? How do I do that when she has made it perfectly clear that I don't mean anything to her?"

"You talk to her. Tell her how you feel and then, even if she does maintain that there's nothing left to work with, you know you tried all you could."

I stared at Gabe and wondered if it was all so simple, when he himself needed a kick up the arse and the assistance of me, Christine and Carrie to see the light.

"This is the voice of experience speaking. All I have today with Carrie is everything and more, but if I had carried on denying it, then I would have lost it all before I'd truly got it."

"Fucking hell, you even speak like a girl now."

He flipped me off and we both laughed.

"How did it feel seeing her enter through the doors and walk down the aisle?" He wasn't taking any prisoners and was going straight for the kill.

"Amazing. She looked fucking phenomenal, and for a second I forgot that she wasn't mine."

"And when she took your arm to follow me and Carrie out?" Yeah, straight for the kill.

"Better than I thought it would. Better than I thought it should."

He stared at me as I hesitated, wondering if I should continue to speak and say the things he probably didn't want or need to know. He continued to look at me, silently encouraging me to say whatever I wanted to.

"Since Bea, when I've been with a woman, I erm…"

He looked startled. "Impotency is nothing to be ashamed of." His words were sincere, and his face was impassive once more.

"What? No! That's not what I was saying. Dickhead." I shuddered at the thought of it and even if I had been, I wouldn't have felt ashamed.

"What then?"

"The only way I can come is by thinking of her. I close my eyes and see her, not the person I'm with."

"Wow. That certainly tells you that you're not over her."

I glared at him. "Really, Dr Freud? Have you considered this kind of work before?"

This time he flicked me double Vs.

"And I have an erection you could hammer nails in with, have done since I saw her and before the night is out, I may actually die of blue balls."

Gabe laughed, but then stifled it. "Sorry."

"So you say, dickhead."

"I am. Look, you have two choices, move on, forget about her and get rid of your erection and blue balls with someone else or you make your move. Fuck, you don't even know why she dumped your arse and that is unacceptable. Dumping you was her prerogative, and her reasons for doing so should be respected, but how can you respect something you're clueless about?"

I knocked back the remaining whiskey in my glass and

pushed my shoulders back. "You, my friend, are absolutely fucking right. So, tonight, one way or another I am going to get to the bottom of this whether Princess shagging Bea likes it or not."

Gabe nodded and slapped my back just as Carrie joined us.

"Boys," she said with a smile, already sidling into Gabe's side and embrace.

"Angel," he whispered to her.

I settled with my usual, "Nanny." Then, turning back to my friend, I added, "And goodbye to unwanted erections and blue balls."

Gabe lifted his glass and clinked it against my empty one. "I'll drink to that," he said as I slammed my glass down and went in pursuit of Bea and some answers.

As I strode away, I heard Nanny say to Gabe, "I hope that's not your erection we're saying is unwanted."

My friend laughed and said something I didn't hear, but I did hear Nanny call him lover.

Chapter Eight

Bea

I was having an amazing night, all things considered, and by all things, I meant one thing.

After the first dance the dancefloor had been opened up to everyone and I had a feeling Seb was on his way to me, but he never made it that far. One of Gabe's cousins or something similar got to me first and invited me to dance. I'd felt a mixture of disappointment and relief that he had. He was a nice man, and attractive, but I wasn't looking for anything more than a dance partner at that point.

As we moved around the dancefloor, I witnessed the ovary exploding image of Seb picking Charlotte up and dancing around with her. He spun her and even dipped her while she remained in his arms. I couldn't take my eyes off him, scanning the room over my dance partner's shoulder at every opportunity, only to find each sighting more panty wetting and hormonally challenging than the next.

The evening was moving on and Carrie and I, along with Charlotte, had been dancing up a storm pretty much non-stop. Gabe had been over a few times to check on his wife and daughter, ensuring they both had drinks and were generally okay. As we began throwing the moves of a well-established routine around the floor, I saw Gabe approach his friend. He led him away and got them both a drink.

I attempted to be discreet in my observations, but apart from serious expressions, some laughter and the use of fingers to swear, I was clueless as to what was being said.

"If I didn't know you were the one to ditch Seb, I would swear you were mooning," said Carrie as she did some weird move with her arm.

I frowned at her. "Er, no."

She shrugged. "I saw him talking to the leggy blonde who is one of Gabe's colleagues," she told me.

I was unsure if she was winding me up, trying to get a rise from me, or if he had been pursuing the woman Carrie spoke of, but I didn't like it.

"He's a free agent and I don't care who he talks to."

"I guess. He might have dated her before…"

She was definitely provoking me now, and it worked. "That could probably be applied to half of the female population locally, the half under the age of thirty-five, and do you know what? I don't care, not one iota. I could not give a fuck who he talks to or anything else!"

Carrie cocked her head and then allowed a small, self-satisfied smirk to spread across her face. "I think the lady doth protest too much."

Taking a leaf out of the boy's book, I flipped her off and then stropped as far as the bar where I ordered a double something.

I stood at the bar and got another before the first had even finished travelling down my throat. I turned around and watched the people around me. Charlotte was on the dancefloor with Christine while Noel danced at a more sedate pace with Margaret. Carrie was making her way towards Gabe and Seb. With no clue why or what she was likely to say, I looked away. Was she talking about me? Were they all talking about me and if they were, what were they saying? As my own paranoid sounding thoughts registered, I drained my glass and returned to the dancefloor. With the alcohol having gone to my head, maybe because of the speed with which I drank it, my movements were a little bigger, less controlled and attention seeking.

I had no clue how long I'd been dancing alone for, seconds or minutes. Someone came alongside me. He introduced himself, but I didn't quite catch it. We moved together and our bodies brushed against each other in an inviting and suggestive way. He pulled me to him, ensuring I could feel the hard lines of his body, and everything else. This guy was looking for a good time and maybe I was. I spun around so that my back was against him, my behind pressed to his groin that was certainly looking for a good time, and that is when I saw Seb. No more than ten feet away on the edge of the dancefloor. He glared at me and my dance partner with a look that was murderous.

How dare he? What right did he have to glare? We were not together, and we hadn't been for months. I had no doubt he would have been with other women in that time and I had no reason to think he'd given me any thought.

I turned back and whispered to my partner and then dashed to the DJ where I requested a song, Don't Start Now by Dua Lipa which had started before I got back to the dancefloor.

Seb remained in the same spot and watched me dance, and I hoped listened to the words about if you don't want to see me dance with somebody else, about not coming out and staying in. I ignored the voice inside my head that reminded me that I had been the one to issue the goodbye, not him. I also ignored the feelings of guilt and sorrow, and then, hands came to rest on my hips after they'd skimmed around my body.

I closed my eyes, startled and scared because I did not want this, with this man; the dancing or the one-night stand I was all but certain was on offer. Following a deep breath and a hard swallow, I opened my eyes, prepared to put a stop to this, the dancing and the unkind tormenting of Seb, not that I was sure he was bothered.

The spot where he'd stood was now empty. "Shit!" I looked at the guy I'd been dancing with and began to explain that the dance and everything else was over. "Nice to have met you, but —"

My words were cut off as I wobbled on my heels then realised someone had my arm and was enforcing some distance between me and whatever his name was. Seb.

"We need to talk," he said with a flatness that disturbed me.

I wobbled again.

"Correction, you need to sober up and then we need to talk."

"I don't know what's going on here," said Mr Whatever his

name was.

"Nothing is going on," Seb told him. "Whatever this was is over and won't be happening again."

Like that, he disappeared, leaving me alone with Seb.

We stood, staring at each other. Seb looked furious and although I was unsure how I looked, I felt really, really drunk.

The DJ made an announcement that the bride and groom were leaving. Everyone moved to the sides of the room and clapped and cheered as Carrie and Gabe left the reception, heading for the bridal suite. Charlotte, who was spending the night at the hotel with her grandparents called after them with a succession of mummies and daddies.

As soon as they left, Seb took my hand, scorching me with his touch. "And now, Princess, we are leaving too."

Chapter Nine

Seb

"Where are you taking me?" Bea asked as we stepped into the lift.

"Your room or mine. Either works for me." I was quietly seething. The sight of her dancing and rubbing herself up against that dickhead on the dancefloor had me seeing red. Add to that the audacity of her song choice! How fucking dare she! She was the one to dump me, not the other way around so if anybody should have been told to fucking stay home, it was her.

She stared across at me, very much the worse for wear. "I'm sharing with Carrie."

I shook my head at her, disapproval and annoyance increasing with every word she uttered.

"Not tonight you're not. You stayed with her last night, tonight she is in the bridal suite with Gabe."

She giggled and then whispered, "What do you think they're doing, in the honeymoon suite?"

I arched a brow, unwilling to think about that because apart from anything else my own dick was ramrod hard and the earlier suggestion of blue balls was becoming a reality.

"Carrie has the tiniest, lacy things on underneath her dress—"

"That I don't need to know about. Come on."

We got off at my floor and with her hand in mine, if only to keep her upright, I led Bea to my room. The door had barely closed when I turned to see her bouncing on my bed. Her dress was rucked up, flashing her legs and her boobs were jiggling.

Fucking hell, why didn't I think this through, bringing her here?

"Shall we have a drink?" she asked, but her eyes were searching for the minibar.

Unfortunately for her, I was way ahead of her and was inserting a coffee cartridge into the drinks maker.

"You're having a drink. Several drinks and then we are going to talk and sort this the fuck out once and for all."

She looked startled by my assertion. Typically, I was chilled and laid back, rarely riled, but honestly, since she had unceremoniously dumped my arse, nobody riled me quite like Princess Bea. Yeah, this was out of character for me, and that should ring bells for her, if only she wasn't so fucking shit faced.

The first cup of coffee went down with a few giggles and random snippets of conversation. The second cup went down in near silence and by the time I was making her the third one, she was glaring at me and pouting, but she did at least drink it.

With her sobering up and a hangover most likely beginning to hit, I broached the subject of us. "What happened, Bea, to us?"

She shrugged, that one move causing my temper to rise again.

I stared at her, daring her to maintain her silence now.

"Does it matter?"

She was really pissing me off with every word she uttered. How times had changed. There was a time, such a short time ago when everything she said filled my heart with joy and laughter.

"Yes, it fucking matters!" I snapped. "We were honest from day one, or at least I was and then suddenly with no warning or indication that you were no longer happy, you casually drop into the conversation that you're done."

She looked up at me and did look a little contrite.

"I was done."

I glared at her, rage rolling off me in a red mist of blurred waves. "You were done? You were fucking done? Well that's okay then, sorry to have inconvenienced you!"

She jumped as I leapt up and began to pace the floor.

"We went to dinner, on a date and then we went back to my house where we drank and laughed and went to bed. You let me fuck you, all the time knowing it was goodbye for you and then you dumped me, without a second thought so don't you dare insult me now with, *I was done*. I deserve an explanation beyond that, don't I?"

"Seb, what good will it do to go over it? It won't change things, will it? It won't change who we are?"

I stared at her and as ready as I was to unleash my full wrath onto her, I didn't. She looked regretful, sad, lonely and close to tears.

"Bea." I reached for her, wanting to hold her and offer her some comfort, which was ridiculous considering how much she'd hurt me.

"No, please." She wrapped her own arms around her body, hugging herself.

I wanted to hold her even more. The idea that she sought solace and reassurance from her own arms and not mine, cut me deep, deeper than I thought possible. It hurt me, she'd hurt me, again and yet here I was ready to leap in and put my own thoughts and feelings to one side in order to focus on hers. Moving closer, I pried her arms away and replaced them with my own and pulled her to me, held her close and lay us both down on my bed.

A smile curled my lips when she allowed me to hold her. She nestled into me, her face found a place in my neck and she clung to me. My arms tightened around her, and I rested my lips against her head, "Ssh."

We remained that way for several minutes and then, her breathing slowed until we both fell asleep, together.

****

I opened my eyes and was dazzled by daylight and sun flooding the room. The sensation of my arms and bed being empty registered and I leapt up. Sitting bolt upright I saw Bea standing at the door. She looked slightly startled when our eyes met. I wasn't sure what to say, what I could say, but I didn't need to.

"I didn't dump you without a second thought, Seb. You were all I thought about until I wasn't sure I'd be able to take my next breath without you. I'm still not, and that is why I ended things, because I knew that wasn't what you wanted." Tears rose in her eyes, but she held them back, contained them. "I seriously considered just carrying on, but after that night, I knew that if I didn't do it then, when it eventually ended it would destroy me. It came pretty close this time."

I stared at her positioned at the door with her hand ready to open it and leave, the first of her tears overflowing her eyes.

"Bea—" I began but she cut me off.

"I broke our promise, our pinky promise, the first one. We agreed, no expectations, no sentiment nor feelings, but I broke it by falling head over heels in love with you." With the final word a sob escaped her as she pulled the door open.

Chapter Ten

Bea

Why the hell had I just blurted that out? Although, at least he would leave me the fuck alone now he knew I'd developed feelings, mushy, soft, loving feelings. I didn't know much about Seb, but he'd been clear on his thoughts on those pesky *feelings.*

With one foot put forward, I seemed to lose my balance, so much so that I was sure my backwards fall would only be broken by the floor. It wasn't. I wasn't falling. Seb was pulling me back, back into the room and clear of the door that swung shut. Immediately, I felt myself pressed against the wall and then, as if in slow motion, Seb's mouth lowered to mine and kissed me.

I was lost in his kiss and embrace immediately, and never wanted it to end. I had missed this, I had missed him, but was scared because I didn't know what this was, nor what it meant to Seb. And now that I'd had another taste of this, I wouldn't be able to go back to a life without it.

Seb's arms wrapped around me, one landed on my behind and the other came to rest between my shoulder blades and then I was moving. He was carrying me, not stopping until he was placing me on the bed. He pulled back and briefly broke our kiss that had felt like I was being devoured.

"Tell me to stop, Princess. If you don't want me, want this, tell me to stop, now."

I shook my head. "I want you, but I'm scared."

He leaned down and ran a hand through my hair. "You don't

need to be scared. I won't hurt you."

I gazed up at him and didn't doubt what he was saying, physically anyway, but that wasn't what I feared.

"Is this...well, I don't know what I'm asking. You haven't said anything to what I said about why I ended things."

"No, I haven't. I wish you'd told me at the time how you were feeling."

I looked down, feeling awkward and embarrassed.

"Hey, Princess." He tilted my chin up so I was looking at him. "We'll talk."

"But I broke our pinky promise, feelings were not supposed to be part of this and as I'm the only one with them—"

My words were stemmed with another assault of my mouth by his.

"And who said you were the only one catching feelings?"

I stared at him and held my breath, was he saying what I thought he was? What should I say in response?

He carried on without me. "Nobody said that because it was never a conversation we had, was it? What did you think I would have done if you'd told me? Run for the hills? Thrown you out of my house? I'm not a complete bastard, and strangely enough, I'm not heartless."

"Sorry." I had nothing else to offer him.

My phone rang and I scrambled to find it, I could see the readout on my screen, it was Christine. I answered. "Oh, no, I'm not there. I'm on my way so I will see you at breakfast. Okay, yeah, five minutes."

"Breakfast time?"

"Yeah. Christine couldn't get an answer from my room."

We both laughed and as the laughter died the atmosphere and apprehension between us amplified.

"Seb, kiss me."

No more words were needed as our mouths melded together. Our lips, caressed, the kind of kiss that was as soft as feathers but could render you breathless. My dress had ridden up and my bare legs wrapped around Seb's middle. His kisses began to travel along my jaw, down my neck and chest before he reached my covered breasts. With his hands grappling with the fabric, desperately searching for a way in, I laughed.

"I'm not laughing here." He looked frustrated to have been thwarted in his efforts.

"The zip is concealed down the back. Do you want me to roll over?"

He arched a brow and smiled. "Nothing I want more, but if you roll over and your arse is in the air while I remove your clothes, we'll be lucky to make dinner, never mind breakfast."

I laughed and with my arms around his neck pulled him back in for a more chaste kiss. "As much as the idea of missing breakfast and lunch with you appeals, I don't particularly want Christine or the bridal party hunting us down."

"You are so fucking wise, my Princess Bea." He kissed my nose and got to his feet. Helping me to mine, he escorted me to the door. "Go back to your room, get changed and I'll do the same here before we go to breakfast. Then, once we're all packed, I'll drive you back and we can talk some more and not be interrupted."

I grinned, and unsure what else to say, but with my mouth drying, I licked my lips.

"For fuck's sake, wench, go, go now." He spun me towards the door, landed a single small spank to my behind then opened the door and guided me through it.

I headed down the corridor, a definite spring in my step as I went and there was only one reason for that. He wanted me. He was taking me home where he would talk some more with me, without interruption, and I couldn't bloody wait.

Chapter Eleven

Seb

Immediate family had all stayed in the hotel they'd assembled for breakfast, including the newlyweds. Gabe looked happy, relaxed and above all else, bloody smug! He'd clearly had a very good night. Carrie looked happy, she glowed, but honestly, I was unsure if that was down to her newly married status or her recently shagged one. I opted for the latter. Watching on, I saw Gabe whisper something to his wife and then she blushed crimson. Yeah, her glow was sex induced for sure.

Bea and I were the last to arrive and our appearance together caused several knowing glances and raised eyebrows. Yes, we had spent the night together, but beyond some kissing and sleeping nothing had happened, yet.

Charlotte chatted to everyone in turn. She then looked around and announced, "Mummy and Daddy are going on honeymoon, without me."

She had grinned when she'd said Mummy but was scowling by the time she'd said without me. I smirked as I remembered her thinking the honeymoon was actually a trip to the moon.

"And you are going on holiday with Grandma and Grandad," Gabe reminded her.

She pouted.

"Where are you going?" I asked Charlotte, hoping to excite her about her own holiday and distract her from her upset at not going with Gabe and Carrie.

"What's it called again?" she asked her grandparents.

"We are going to have a week in the sun, Portugal, and then visit a certain big eared rodent in Paris," Noel said and while Charlotte frowned at the last part, I knew exactly what that meant, Euro Disney.

I also knew that Gabe had booked seven nights in The Maldives and five further days in Paris, so they'd enjoy some of Charlotte's time there together.

"Wow, that sounds better than some boring old honeymoon," I told Charlotte, forcing a smile from her.

Gabe and Carrie both looked across at me and smiled.

"That sounds amazing," Bea said. "If you don't want to go to Portugal, I will go instead. I need some sun on me."

Those words had me imagining Bea in next to no clothes, sunning herself. Her skin glistening with a combination of some cream, the sea and sweat. Fuck, how I'd make her sweat. My thoughts were not helping the excruciating pain of a still hard dick and aching balls.

Charlotte laughed. "No, I want to go." With a big smile, she was happy again and maybe even looking forward to her holiday.

"I love Paris. It holds such precious memories for us, doesn't it, lover?" Margaret was suddenly back with us at the mention of Paris.

Gabe got up and walked down to where his grandmother sat. He leaned down and gently kissed her cheek. "It certainly does, you little minx."

She giggled and blushed.

"But ssh, we don't want everyone to know our secrets, do we?" He kissed her again and then retook his seat next to Carrie.

Christine looked relieved that her mother hadn't shared any more intimate memories of her marriage to her father.

Breakfast was easy and relaxed, although as Bea was about halfway through her full English, she began to look a little green. But then, why wouldn't she? From what I'd seen she had eaten very little the day before and when I factored in the amount of alcohol she'd downed, she must be suffering the after effects of that, if not a full-blown hangover.

Gabe and Carrie were heading to the airport straight from the hotel that afternoon, but the rest of us had a noon checkout and were returning home. Originally, Bea had been going back with Christine but now she would be travelling with me.

The table dispersed and as I helped Margaret to her feet and offered her my arm, she glanced up at me, a definite glimmer in her eyes.

"Have you ever been to Paris, darling?"

I arched a brow.

"We should go, you and I."

I smiled down at her but said nothing.

"It would be a trip you'd never forget. I guarantee it."

With a laugh, I replied. "I don't doubt that you sorceress, you."

She blushed adoringly. "My first time with bondage was in Paris, you know."

I nodded. We all knew that. Fortunately, Christine was out of earshot with Charlotte. Not Noel though, who shook his head with a smile.

"And anal."

We all knew that too.

"And my first ménage."

I stopped abruptly and almost knocked her over with that revelation.

She looked up at me and I wondered how this vibrant, sexy, liberated and beautiful woman had become so confused with a brain that didn't cooperate and function as it once had. She had adored her husband and him her, and now she confused her own grandson for him. I began to think how cruel life was and then I realised that the alternative to this, for a coherent and lucid Margaret, would be to have all these memories combined with grief for her beloved and nobody to share them with. Maybe this was better, in a strange way.

"Margaret." Noel stood at her other side to escort her back to her room.

She took the arm he offered but kept hold of mine. "Come on then boys. Paris awaits."

We smiled at each other across the top of her head.

"You, Margot, are going to get me into lots and lots of

trouble," I told her, unsure why I had called her Margot, although this minx persona was more Margot than Margaret.

"You're welcome." She giggled as we entered the lift.

****

I was all packed up and ready to go. I'd got back to my room and showered and shaved before redressing in jeans and a white t-shirt. With a final tour of the room, I was happy I hadn't forgotten anything so made my way to the foyer to find Gabe and Carrie sitting and drinking coffee.

"Hey, Mr and Mrs," I called.

They both looked up and gestured for me to join them.

"You and Bea are the last ones to go," Carrie told me.

I looked around for Bea, but there was no sign.

"She's not down yet. She's a little fragile," Carrie explained.

"Well she should have taken it easy last night, she was knocking it back before we left," Gabe chipped in.

"Yeah, well…" I had nothing else to offer.

"What happened with you two last night?" Carrie's question caused Gabe to frown at her.

"Angel," he warned.

"I was only asking, baby," she replied with the sweetest smile that removed any objections Gabe might have had.

I shook my head at him. "Pussy."

He flipped me off. "Yeah, I think that was my wife's question. Get any?"

Carrie smacked his arm but giggled.

"How are your blue balls, by the way?" my friend asked, and I couldn't help but laugh and answer.

"Big, heavy and almost navy in colour, thanks for asking."

He laughed while Carrie looked on aghast. "Oh my God, TMI."

We both laughed at her.

"Maybe not for long." Gabe nodded behind me and when I turned. I came face to face with Bea.

Fuck me, she looked beautiful. Her hair was damp and her face free of all make-up. She wore a white sundress that had an orange and yellow floral print. On her feet she wore flat brown sandals, and nobody had ever looked more attractive to me. She looked a little less fragile than earlier, maybe just tired. I was unsure, if given the opportunity to lie down whether I would be capable of letting her sleep.

She came to a standstill next to me. "Ready?"

I was more than ready, for this trip home, for talking, for everything, including getting rid of my blue balls.

Gabe gave me a knowing look while Carrie leaned in and kissed my cheek, then Bea's. "Be careful, both of you. If I come back from honeymoon and you've fucked it up again, there'll be hell to pay," she warned.

Gabe rolled his eyes. "Is this you keeping out of it?" They had clearly had this conversation already.

She looked at him and shrugged.

I was determined not to fuck it up, not again.

Chapter Twelve

Bea

We had barely left the hotel grounds when my eyes became heavy and I lost the battle to sleep. I didn't realise that until I woke up and found Seb pulling into a service area on a tiny 'B' road that was virtually deserted. We got out of the car and I was glad to stretch my legs. We went into the shop and grabbed what was essentially a picnic, sandwiches, crisps, chocolate biscuits, soft drinks, and coffee from a vending machine. Instead of going back to the car, Seb led us around the back of the garage where there was a picnic area around a lake and a wooded area beyond.

Sat opposite each other at a wooden picnic table, we began to eat and drink.

"Gabe and Carrie looked ridiculously happy." I smiled, pleased for them both.

Seb nodded and smiled. "They really did, and Charlotte, apart from her disappointment at not getting an invitation to the honeymoon!" His face morphed into a small grimace.

I laughed. "I'd happily take a week in Portugal and Paris."

His mouth opened and closed a couple of times, but no words were uttered so I moved on.

"And Margaret."

We both laughed. "I hope to grow old disgracefully, just like her."

I shook my head. "I have no doubt you will."

"Does Nanny suspect about The Maldives?"

"No. She was thinking somewhere sunny and hot, but beyond

that she hasn't said anything." I smiled at his Nanny name for Carrie.

Seb nodded. "He just wanted something special for the two of them."

I smiled. I loved what Gabe had planned for my friend and that he was kind and thoughtful. Looking across at Seb, I wondered if he would do something as considerate for his wife. I pushed that thought from my mind as quickly as it had entered it. No good would come of thinking of him that way, of comparing him to Gabe, moreover, comparing my relationship with him to Carrie's with Gabe, even if I was a little envious of it.

"I don't know Carrie well, in terms of time, not like you and Gabe, but she hasn't always had that, someone doing right by her, so as her friend it's good to see." I returned my focus to our friends and reorganised my mind so that there were no thoughts of Seb, marriage, me and honeymoon together.

"I don't think you need to have known someone for a long time to be a good friend or know them."

I nodded my genuine agreement.

"Gabe's story is not mine to tell but he was well overdue some luck and someone to do right by him for a long time, too, so let's drink to them finding each other and being sickeningly happy together."

We made to clink our padded cardboard coffee cups together. "Cheers," we said in unison.

"What do you want to do? About us? From me?"

I looked up, startled, and wondered how long he'd been thinking of these garbled questions that were random in their timing. Judging by the speed of the words leaving his mouth, they'd been building up a while.

The temptation was to simply repeat them back. What did he want to do? About us? From me?

If I knew his answers to my questions then I would know how to reply, but I didn't, so what should I do? I could guess what I thought he wanted me to say or I could be honest. Guessing could backfire, so I went with honesty.

"I don't know, not really. I enjoyed what we had, and I had no plans to develop feelings for you..."

"Yeah, those pesky feelings will do that, won't they? Creep up on you with no warning, fuckers."

I laughed at his words, because they were completely true, certainly where me and Seb were concerned.

"Yeah, that. I want to try again and to make it work. Not Gabe and Carrie and marriage and babies kind of work, necessarily, but for us to make this work for both of us."

He nodded. "Okay, so exclusive, monogamous, relationship kind of stuff."

"Yes."

He smiled. "With some of those fuzzy feelings and shit?"

"If possible." I grinned across at him.

"Hand holding, kissing, fooling around and very hot and dirty fucking?"

I panted at the thought, the memory of all those things coursed through me. I really had missed sex and sex with Seb was like nothing I'd ever known. "Yes, definitely."

"You have yourself a deal, Princess, on one condition."

My heart sank, clueless as to what he was about to say. Was he putting a time on it or making this a secret? "Go on."

"You never fucking cut and run without speaking to me first, do you understand?"

It sounded as though I was being told off. As if he was genuinely angry with me and his expression kind of backed that up.

"Yes."

"Promise."

"I promise." I meant it.

He shook his head. "Pinky promise." He extended his little finger. "And remember, if you break a second pinky promise, all the unicorns in the world get chronic diarrhoea and die messy and horrible deaths, so unless you want that on your conscience..." He shrugged.

My laughter rang around us before I linked my pinky finger with his and shook it. "Pinky promise, babe."

"Thank fuck for that, because Charlotte would never forgive you for the unicorns alone."

I collected our rubbish and deposited it in a nearby dustbin.

When I turned. Seb stood right before me.

"I think we should seal the deal with a kiss."

"A kiss?" I quirked an eyebrow.

"Hmmm, and maybe some hand holding."

I nodded.

He took my hand is his and leaned in to kiss my lips gently. "I'm thinking we might need some fooling around too."

I felt myself flush but couldn't deny that I was on board with this plan we were devising. "And what about very hot and dirty fucking?"

"That depends. I am totally up for all of that, but I should warn you that if you don't turn around and head back towards the car, all of that will be happening somewhere al fresco and secluded over there." He pointed towards the lake, trees and beyond.

The ball was now firmly in my court. I got to decide what happened and when. I had no doubt what Seb wanted. His desire for me had been ramrod hard every time we'd touched.

I looked up and smiled then turned my back on him. Reaching behind I took his hand in mine and with a small bite into my lower lip I replied, "I think I'd like to take a closer look at the lake, and the trees, and your blue balls."

"Fucking hell, Princess, you are well and truly fucked."

"I'm hoping to be."

He cocked his head at me. I dropped his hand and began to run in the opposite direction to the car. "Catch me if you can," I called over my shoulder and saw him laugh.

"Yup, fucked six ways from Sunday, Princess."

Chapter Thirteen

Seb

Within about three strides I had caught her and thrown her over my shoulder. I ran as fast as my legs could carry me until we came to a copse of trees near the far side of the lake. I placed Bea down as gently as I could considering I was about three seconds from throwing her down and stripping her bare.

Her hands were full of my shirt, enabling her to encourage me down with her by pulling me lower. I didn't really need much encouragement. I wanted this, no, *needed* it, I needed her like I needed my next breath.

Leaning back, kneeling between her legs that she'd spread to accommodate me, I pulled my top off over my head. Looking back at her she was already undoing the buttons that ran the length of her dress revealing a white lace bra that did nothing to disguise her heaving breasts or stiff nipples that seemed to shine through the fabric.

I couldn't take my eyes of her as more and more flesh was revealed; her ribs, the softness of her belly, the curve of her hips and then her freshly waxed sex.

"You appear to have forgotten your underwear, Princess."

I was fucking salivating at the sight of her.

She shrugged and then offered me a cheeky little smirk. "I was kind of hoping to avoid any unnecessary delays."

"Delays?"

"Yeah, delays in us being naked and fucking."

I laughed. "Good plan. I'm impressed. But I'm not sure I

approve of no knickers." The truth was I very much approved of her lack of knickers. I might just insist that she never wore them when we were together.

"Maybe you should punish me."

I stared down at her and remembered having spanked her a couple of times, nothing heavy and only during sex.

"Maybe I should, but not now because I need to be inside you more than anything else."

"Hurry up then," she snapped, pulling her bra down so her breasts were being pushed up by the fabric before spreading her thighs even wider.

My hand was already on my waistband, undoing the button and then the zip. I pushed my jeans and underwear down in one, releasing my hard, engorged dick and my balls that were heavy and fucking painful.

She licked her lips.

"Not a fucking chance. I need to be inside your tight little pussy, and soon."

Bea was undoubtedly the sexiest woman I had ever known. She was the sort of girl you'd take home to your mum without question, but alone, behind closed doors, or in this case outdoors, she was something else entirely. She was sensual and so responsive to my words and touch. Her love of sex was undeniable, and she knew exactly how to gain pleasure and satisfaction. Her confidence in the pursuit of her own pleasure and giving me mine had been the biggest turn on I had ever known.

"And I need you inside me, so hurry the fuck up."

I looked down at her and laughed. Yeah, her confidence was something else. Lowering my gaze, I watched her hand skimming down the expanse of her exposed skin until it came to settle between her legs. I watched on, mesmerised at the sight before me. She slipped a finger inside herself, then a second, before sliding it up to her clit that she began to circle, slowly at first and then faster until her breathing hitched. Her other hand was alternating between each breast, cupping it and then pinching the nipple causing her to arch her back and moan.

I leaned down, sinking one of my fingers inside her and then a second while she continued to circle her clit. I could feel how close she was to her release when her muscles contracted, and moisture coated my digits.

"Seb, fuck!" she cried, edging closer to her climax.

I pulled her hand from her clit and drew her fingers into my mouth, sucking them clean. Then I removed my own nectar covered ones and almost lost my mind as I sucked them hard, savouring every last drop of her.

Leaning down, my body blanketed hers. My mouth found her breasts, sucking, licking and biting her nipples until she thrashed around beneath me. Slowly, I slid my dick inside her, and fuck, if that didn't feel like the best place in the whole fucking world. It was like this is where I was meant to be, inside this woman.

I began moving, slowly at first and then faster. My lips moved up her chest, neck, ear and mouth until we were kissing like our lives depended on it. Her whole body shook and pulsed around me as she moved ever closer to release.

"Shit, Princess, I am going to come. Come with me, come on," I hissed through gritted teeth, increasing the speed of my movements, brushing against her clit with every stroke.

She exploded beneath me and as she thrashed around, arching her back and crying my name, she took me there with her. I had never known sexual pleasure and gratification like it, and it was also fucking excruciating too, but at least now, my blue balls were no more.

Chapter Fourteen

Bea

The smile I was wearing was beginning to make my face hurt. It had been there since the day after Carrie's wedding and now, almost two weeks later, it was still there. Seb and I had seen each other every day since and things just kept getting better.

Work had been busy as the family I worked for had a few issues, with both parents working extra-long hours and the mum going away for several days on business. I'd been working slightly longer hours and if the parents had got their way, I would have been working twenty-four-seven. I recollected when Carrie worked for Gabe and how her evenings and weekends were hers to do with as she saw fit and wondered how the parents I worked for would cope if either were a one parent family as Gabe had been. That seemed even more ironic when I considered the fact that Carrie had lived in, I didn't. I appreciated my own place and space.

The sound of my intercom buzzing broke my thoughts. The sound of Seb's voice made my smile broaden and as I released the door, I looked around my home. It was nothing special. A fairly standard one-bedroom studio. An old Victorian house a couple of streets from where I worked, in the attic. I recalled how embarrassed I was the first time Seb came here; my home is comfortable and clean, but I was overly aware that he had money and was a friend of Gabe's who also had money. His house was huge, big enough that there was a self-contained flat for his nanny on the top floor of his house. I wasn't sure what Seb would make of my home, but I needn't have worried because from the first time he'd entered it, he had been nothing but comfortable.

Seb lived in a very nice house. It was luxurious with a garden and a terrace, two bathrooms, a home gym and office as well as two bedrooms. It was a very nice bachelor pad, although he'd often told me he didn't use it as, and I quote, a shag palace.

A tap at the door signalled his arrival. I opened it and grinned to see him standing there, breathing heavily, exaggeratingly so.

"You should charge people to visit you, like a gym because it's a serious workout getting up here."

I leaned in, as if to kiss him. "I was hoping for a slightly different workout but if you're not the man for the job." I turned away, throwing a smirk at him over my shoulder.

"Not a fucking chance of any other man being the one for the job, now get your arse over here and kiss me."

"Catch me if you can." Those five words were becoming my catchphrase since that day at the side of the lake.

I screamed as he leapt towards me, not that I objected to his pursuit or him catching me, none whatsoever. I only got as far as the sofa before he had grabbed my arm, pulled me back and was covering my mouth with his.

****

With Seb's t-shirt covering me up, I prepared some food, cheese, meat, crackers and fruit. It was already after ten and although hungry, too late for anything heavy. Seb wore just his jeans as he took a seat opposite me at my tiny table in the kitchen.

"How was your day?" he asked.

I loved this. Normal conversation. I loved more the fact that he didn't ask me because it was polite or expected, nor did he ask because he couldn't think of anything else to say. He asked because he cared and was interested.

"Meh." I grabbed a handful of grapes and popped them into my mouth.

"That good, huh?"

I shrugged, unsure what to say about my day.

"Come on, tell Uncle Seb."

I laughed and shook my head. "Er, no, never." I shuddered. "Uncle Seb makes you sound like that weird uncle who is a little too touchy."

He laughed. "I am very touchy and plan on touching you again before we go to sleep but not in the weird uncle way, so you'd better just tell plain old Seb."

"There's something going on with the Walkers. You know things have been strained, but Sophie has just returned from business and told me when I was leaving that she's unlikely to be around for the next few weeks."

"Okay," Seb said with a frown. "And..."

"She asked me to keep an eye on the children and to make sure they have everything they need in her absence. She was weird."

"But they're not your children...they're hers and her husband's."

I nodded. "Yeah. Like I say it was weird and then when Maurice came home he was lovely with the children and asked me how I was and how my day was, but completely ignored his wife, as if she wasn't even there."

"Oh dear."

"Yeah. So that was my day and when I took the kids to the park, I missed Carrie and Charlotte."

He laughed at my admission.

"Some of the other nannies were there but it's not the same."

"Oh, Princess, are you missing your bestie?"

"I am," I admitted, thinking she'd been gone almost two weeks and was due back soon.

"Nanny will be back tomorrow, and you can play catch-up, and in the meantime, I will take your mind off missing her, okay?"

I grinned across at him. "You've been doing a good job of that so far. Maybe I can take your mind off missing Gabe."

He laughed loudly at that and shook his head firmly. "Er, no, that's not the way we do things. We don't miss each other and can't wait to be reunited again."

It was my turn to laugh at him now. "Yeah, if you say so. I

see you with your far-off expression. You and Gabe are the greatest bromance of all time."

"If you keep spouting this shit, I am going to put my dick in your mouth to stop you speaking at all."

I stared across at him and licked my lips slowly and seductively.

"Fill up," he said, pointing to the food in front of us. "Before I fill you up."

Chapter Fifteen

Seb

Things were weird. I couldn't quite put my finger on it, but something was off with Bea. It had been a couple of days since we'd spent the night at hers and she'd told me about her employers, who it seemed were having marital problems if not separating. I hoped that's all it was, that work was a little stressy and maybe just odd as she readjusted. She had missed Carrie who was her closest friend. Since Nanny had been attacked by a mutual friend, acquaintance, Bea had rethought a lot of her relationships and adjusted them, distanced herself a little, which I thought was understandable under the circumstances.

Now that our friends were back from their honeymoon, I hoped she might settle down again, in her work, her friendships and our relationship because God knows I really was growing accustomed to us being together.

We were supposed to see each other tonight, but her boss, Maurice, had encountered an emergency at work and needed her to take care of the children. I couldn't deny how pissed off I was about that, but she had told me it really was unavoidable and as his wife was away, Maurice's hands were tied. I wasn't convinced, but that could have just been because I was pissed off at missing my Princess Bea fix.

I'd made her promise that under no circumstances would she agree to any work over the weekend, no matter what emergency, and I had a very sneaky suspicion, Maurice would encounter an emergency. She had sounded disappointed to cancel our plans tonight and I knew she was desperate to visit Gabe, Carrie and Charlotte which is what our plan was for the following day.

We'd text for most of the early evening, nothing of note, banter, chat and although there had been some flirtations that were beginning to move into sexting territory, there was nothing too gratuitous or outrageous, after all, Bea was still working.

My last message had referred to her never making it as a vegetarian due to her love of having meat in her mouth, my meat. There had been no reply after that and as it was now after ten o'clock, I was getting irritated. This was unlike her. She didn't ignore messages and as such her replies were rarely delayed. In fact, I couldn't remember an occasion when her replies had taken more than a few minutes. I struggled to shift the feeling that there was a reason for the lack of a response and I was certain that Bea was deliberately choosing not to reply.

I checked my phone, again. "Fuck!" I was pacing the floor, rolling my phone in my hand and fighting every urge to phone her and demand to know where she was and what she was doing. Precisely, I wanted to know if she was deliberately ignoring me, and even if she wasn't, why hadn't she replied? I was rarely ignored and when on the odd occasions when I had been, I hadn't liked it, not one bit. It brought back bad memories along with the irritation and uncomfortable feeling.

I needed to do something that didn't involve staring at my phone, willing it to ring or something. After a couple of huffs and mutterings to myself, I decided to have a shower and then, if she hadn't made contact. I would phone her.

The shower was hot, just how I liked it, and although I didn't take too much time in there I did try and relax a little before getting out and wrapping a towel around my middle. I made my way back into the lounge where I'd left my phone, relieved to see a message from Bea.

"Thank fuck."

I opened the message and although glad to have heard from her I was slightly miffed to have missed its arrival and then more annoyed when I saw what it said.

<Sorry babe, things got busy, but am all done and just got

home. Am knackered so off to bed. See you tomorrow x>

Well, what the fuck was that all about? Things got busy, what things? Plus, why was she only just getting home from her day that started at seven that morning? I wasn't happy, and although I was going to reply to her, I knew she probably wouldn't respond because her message landed nine minutes ago, and she'd said she was going to bed.

<Princess, I was getting ready to find you. We'll talk about it tomorrow. Night, sweetheart, sleep tight x>

****

Sleep was elusive and by half five the following morning I was already up, preparing to kill time until it was a suitable hour to contact Bea. I made a cup of tea, turned the radio on, then off, turned the TV on, then off before deciding to go and put some time in on the treadmill or something.

I was bathing in sweat by the time half seven came. The shower was my next stop and then breakfast before I ran out of patience and contacted my girlfriend. I shuddered then laughed at myself thinking of naming things and giving each other labels.

With a bacon sandwich and another cup of tea to hand, I grabbed my phone and decided to message her, to start with.

<Morning, Princess. Hope you slept well. Shall I come for you at 12 if we're getting to Gabe's for 1? X>

I stared at my phone, both willing her to reply and daring her not to. My message went from sent to seen and I felt a smile curve my lips.

<*Morning babe. Slept ok, hope you did too. Yeah 12 works for me x>*

<I slept like shit. I missed you in my bed or being in yours. I plan on spending the whole weekend with you now

and I can't wait. X>

<I missed you too. C u at 12 x>

What I'd wanted was for her to reply and not to be offhand or aloof, and both objectives had been met. So, why the hell did I have a horrible feeling in the pit of my stomach that something wasn't right? Was it still due to her late finish? Was it that she hadn't replied last night, although I knew she was going straight to bed, she'd told me that? Or was it that this morning she wasn't her usual chatty self? We'd just made our plan for the day, she'd agreed to it and with the exception of a few comments like missing me, asking how I'd slept and calling me babe, she'd been happy to end our communication. She was always up for a chat, especially at the weekend, although we normally woke up together.

"Pull yourself together, man." I headed to the bedroom to find some clothes to wear for my day with Bea. An afternoon that would be spent with my friends and Charlotte, my family.

Chapter Sixteen

Bea

There were a few hours before Seb would be arriving, so, after a broken night's sleep, I opted to go back to bed with a cup of tea before showering and dressing, it was Saturday morning after all.

Waking, I realised I had slept a little longer than I'd planned but was confident I could still be ready before Seb's arrival, and I was. It was a lovely summer day so I dressed in a pair of stone coloured shorts and a white vest. My hair was up in a high ponytail and when my intercom sounded, I was slipping on white pumps.

I opened the front door so Seb could come in when he got upstairs while I grabbed my phone and purse to throw into my bag.

"Hey, sexy lady," he called, possibly before he'd even seen me.

As I reached his side, he pulled me to him and leaned in to kiss me.

"Hello." I reached up and ran my fingers through his hair, loving how safe I felt in his embrace.

He gazed down, his eyes raked my body from head to toe and back up again. "Nice shorts." He wiggled his eyebrows, making me laugh.

"Right back at you." I slipped my hand into a pocket of the soft, jersey shorts he'd teamed with a white-t-shirt.

"If you don't remove your hand from my pocket, we aren't

leaving the bed all weekend."

A little reluctantly, I pulled my hand out and let it drop to my side.

"Later, my pockets are all yours," he told me with a smile and another kiss that he placed on my lips. "Now, come on or Gabe and Nanny will have eaten without us and I am starving."

We pulled up outside Carrie and Gabe's house and before I'd closed my door, their front door was bursting open. Charlotte was rushing down the steps towards Seb while her parents stood in the open doorway looking happy, tanned and relaxed. Gabe had an arm around Carrie's waist so that his hand rested on her hip, protectively and possessively.

I laughed as Seb scooped Charlotte up and littered dozens of kisses to her face as she fidgeted and giggled.

"I have missed you so much," he told her, melting my heart a little more. "You can't ever go away for so long without me again."

I'd seen Seb with Charlotte countless times and there was no mistaking his love for her. He absolutely adored her, and it was entirely mutual. Watching their interaction I suddenly saw him for the first time as a future father. In fact, that was all I could see in the scene before me. Seb would make a wonderful dad, but was that going to be to my children? I hoped so and as I was sure I felt my ovaries popping, they clearly agreed.

Once we got to the front door, we all exchanged hugs before entering the house. Carrie put the kettle on, and I followed her to the kitchen while the boys and Charlotte went through to the garden.

"How's married life treating you, Mrs Caldwell?"

She smirked at my use of her married name.

"Amazingly." Her smirk became a smile that got bigger until it turned into a grin. "I have actually never been so happy in my whole life as I am now. But what about you? You look tired...or should I draw my own conclusions on why that might be?" She wiggled her eyebrows suggestively and we both laughed.

My face turned serious as I began to explain. "Work is awkward, tense...this has to stay between us."

She nodded.

"Maurice and Sophie have split up. She has gone away for a few weeks to get her head together and the children have stayed behind with him."

"Aww, that's sad," said Carrie, adding water to cups. "So why is this a secret?" She was suspicious now.

"That bit's not, kind of. So, she has gone to find herself or whatever and asked me to take care of the children. He has intimated that their marriage has been rocky for a while and that Sophie may have strayed, but not with another man."

"Ah."

"I mean, I wouldn't want their life to become gossip and then there's the children."

Carrie nodded again but could sense there was more to come.

"He came home late last night. I had agreed to stay with the children until he returned and when he did, he was drunk, really drunk. He made a clumsy pass at me, saying he hadn't had sex in two years and then he passed out."

"Shit! Are you okay?"

I loved that her first concern was for me. I nodded.

"How dare he do that to you, to anyone." She was fuming as she continued. "Did he hurt you, touch you?" She was heading towards me, ready to comfort me.

I loved Carrie, she was still thinking of me and my wellbeing even as she got angrier with my boss. I knew that much of her concern and fury stemmed from her own experience of being on the receiving end of Toby's attack on her, his assault, attempted date rape.

"I'm fine. It was nothing, well, not nothing, but he wasn't threatening."

She didn't look convinced. "If you're sure."

"I am."

"If he does this again or you ever feel unsafe there, you leave. No questions, no putting the children first. You promise you put you first."

I nodded. "I promise." I leaned in and hugged her tight, loving the friend she was and thanked my lucky stars to have her in my life.

She softened slightly as she changed her focus. "I bet he feels awkward this morning."

"I don't know if he remembers. I told Seb I'd worked late, which I did, but I also told him I got home and was going to bed. I stayed over until Maurice woke up at five this morning and was hungover but capable of caring for the children."

"Shit. I'm sure Seb would have understood that—"

"Not without me telling him about the pass and he would not have understood that. If I'd told him about everything else and not that it would have been dishonest whereas one white lie about what time I left felt more truthful."

"I guess. Please be careful with Maurice. I meant what I said about if he says or does anything again, promise you will tell me and leave immediately."

I nodded at her again and then laughed. "I hope Maurice doesn't know that we're friends and assumes I am looking for my own Gabe."

"Fuck!" she cried. "I am a cliché, my marriage, family and life is one big cliché!"

"And a beautiful cliché it is too." Gabe stood in the doorway. "Come on, Angel. I'm getting lonely without you."

"But you have your first love back in your life." She grinned up at her husband, teasing him, much as I'd teased Seb about their bromance.

"I said, I'm getting lonely without you, and as much as I enjoy Seb's company, he lacks your appeal and charm."

"Appeal and charm? Is that code for my boobs and arse?"

Gabe was already pulling her close, both of his hands cupping her behind. "Appeal and charm might be code for a whole lot more."

They were now oblivious to my presence.

"Aww, baby. How will you manage when you go back to work?"

"I have absolutely no clue," he said as he tightened his hold on her and their lips were on a collision course for each other.

I snuck out of the kitchen and made my way outside to where Seb and Charlotte were playing with dolls, and then my ovaries went off again.

Chapter Seventeen

Seb

Bea came back outside to re-join me and was followed shortly after by Carrie and Gabe who were sickeningly happy. We barbecued, laughed, chatted and had a couple of drinks, passing the afternoon quickly and pleasurably.

Charlotte had enjoyed her trip to Portugal but had enjoyed the trip to Disneyland more. She told us detail after detail while Carrie told us how amazing The Maldives and Paris itself had been. I ribbed her a few times about Paris, and she flushed while Gabe gave me warning glances before ending up laughing at his wife's flustered embarrassment. I didn't doubt that both Gabe's wife and grandmother now had the best of memories from the French capital.

As we moved from the garden, where Carrie and Bea had spent time jumping around on the trampoline, into the house, I noticed several wedding photos had already appeared. There was one of Gabe and Carrie coming back up the aisle as a married couple and in the shot, you could see me and Bea behind them. I was gazing down at her adoringly and she had her head cast down slightly, and although the shot was black and white, I swear I could see the pink hue on her cheeks.

"What an attractive quartet we are," I said as an observation more than anything.

The others laughed, but I was serious, we were.

"I need a poo," announced Charlotte, already leaving the room to go to the bathroom.

"Are we going to go out on double dates?" Carrie suddenly asked while Gabe muttered under his breath.

"That would be lovely," Bea said, beaming at the notion.

I shrugged and smiled. I was more than happy to go out with my best friend and his wife who happened to be my girlfriend's best friend.

"We also need to do our girly nights, too," Carrie threw in and while I wasn't thrilled at the prospect of it, Gabe looked more opposed to that than me.

"Just let me know when and I'm onboard with that plan." Bea grinned across at her friend who high fived her.

As the girls were so excited with their plans, I decided to have a little fun myself. "We should have a boy's night then."

"If we do it on the same night, we can save on taxi fares and only need a babysitter for one night," Carrie suggested.

Gabe nodded and Bea began discussing the names of bars where cocktails were two for one.

"I was thinking we could go to a gentlemen's club." It had been my intention to have a little fun with the girls, but the look on their faces was priceless.

"Gentlemen's club?" asked Bea who looked fit to burst with annoyance.

Hers paled compared to Carrie's who looked as though she was going to shoot somebody.

"Yes, gentlemen's club." I looked across at Gabe and winked at him. "Maybe the one we went to on your stag night, they gave us a really good deal and threw in a few very sexy extras."

Carrie got to her feet, just as Charlotte called for someone to wipe her bum. She glared at me, then Gabe. "If you ever step foot in one of those places again, I will fucking divorce you without further ado, do I make myself clear?"

I was stunned by her reaction and her anger. She was usually pretty chilled about everything, and if nothing else, she could take a joke. I barely recognised this version of that woman when I looked at the woman in front of me.

Gabe attempted to defend himself, but Nanny, who was seriously overreacting in my mind, wasn't taking any prisoners.

"I said, do I make myself clear?" she repeated and once he

nodded, she turned on me. "And you, being his best friend and godfather to Charlotte will not save you from me cutting your balls off and refusing to have you within a hundred feet of any of us if you ever so much as suggest taking him to one of those places again, do you understand?"

"Yes, sorry," I said, unsure just what I was sorry for.

"Mummy, I need some help to wipe my bum," called Charlotte, again.

Carrie went to her and after staring at me with angry eyes, was followed by Bea.

Gabe leaned over and punched me hard. "You need to tell Carrie that we never went to a fucking gentlemen's club on my stag night, with or without sexy extras."

"Why?" I was still confused what the issue was.

"Because we fucking didn't! You twat."

"She needs to chill about it," I said with a frown and wondered if Nanny had changed once my friend had put a ring on it. She wouldn't be the first, would she?

Gabe sighed loudly and moved closer to me. "Not my story to tell, but before, a long time ago in her past she knew people who may have been involved in that kind of business and she was hurt by it all."

I had no clue what he meant and without him sharing the story that wasn't his to tell I probably never would. "Okay, okay."

****

We drove back to Bea's, where we were staying, and after apologising to Nanny for what felt like dozens of times and swearing on all I held dear that I had been joking, winding her up about the club, she forgave me, *just*, but did tell me that her threat of cutting my balls of and then cutting me off from her family was very real. I didn't know how to feel about that, not the balls bit. Did her words mean that there could be a time, if something happened between me and her, that she could and would take Gabe and in turn Charlotte from me. That scared me, more than anything. He was my oldest and best friend, but it ran so much deeper than that, and Charlotte, well, she was the nearest I had, or would ever have to a child of my own.

"Hey, penny for your thoughts," Bea said, reaching over to place a reassuring hand on my thigh.

"I was just thinking about Nanny earlier. I was joking and usually she's cool about it, but that was like absolute, cold fury."

"Yeah. She doesn't talk much about her past and she has never mentioned her real family to me, but after her reaction it makes you wonder." She paused for a couple of seconds. "Although, you were a dickhead if you thought you were funny making that kind of joke about her new husband's stag night."

I laughed a little and turned my attention to Bea. "Do you forgive me for my ill-timed joke, Princess?"

"Depends."

"On?"

"On whether you'd try to win favour and make it up to me if I said I didn't forgive you."

I laughed. I knew she meant sex. So, like I needed a reason to make it up to her. "Princess, I am happy to pleasure you all fucking night even without making it up to you or winning favour."

"Well in that case there's nothing to forgive."

"Good."

"So, you're going to pleasure me all night?" She sounded doubtful.

"All fucking night or until you beg me to stop, but then I might just do it some more anyway."

We pulled up outside her flat and as soon as the engine was turned off, she was in my lap, kissing me and running her hands through my hair. I was already stiffening beneath her where she rocked across me.

"You like my plan?" I asked but required no reply.

"I love it." She grinned. "When are you planning on starting?"

I laughed at her eagerness. My hands which had come to rest on her legs began to dance up the soft flesh of her inner thigh before stopping at the fabric of her shorts that pressed against her seam. My palm rested there and pressed her gently, causing her to squirm.

"You feel so hot. Burning."

"I am," she gasped, pressing against me.

I kissed her jaw, tracing a path to her ear. "Are you wet for me?"

There was no hesitation from her. "Yes, very, touch me, feel me."

We both jumped and to be honest, almost shit ourselves when there was an authoritative knock on the window. We both turned to find a police officer looking at us. "Everything okay here?"

"Yes, fine," we replied in stereo, although Bea's was more of a whisper that perfectly suited the crimson colour of her embarrassed face. I had no desire to get arrested, but I couldn't hide my amusement at having been busted like a seventeen-year-old with his first car and girlfriend.

"I live here," she explained and pointed to her flat.

"I'm not opposed to outdoor pursuits myself, but I suggest you take this." He pointed to her in my lap. "Indoors."

We both nodded and got out of the car before doing exactly as he'd suggested, if that's what it was.

Chapter Eighteen

Bea

We were still laughing about the police officer by the time we got to my front door, but as I began to open the door the atmosphere and tension between us intensified and thickened. Seb pulled me to him as we crossed the threshold and before I knew it, I was being crushed between the door and his body.

"Hey," Seb said, cradling my head with one hand. "I've missed you, really missed you."

I smiled, loving that he could miss me even though we'd been together for most of the day. "How much?"

He gave me a dazzling smile and a little shake of his head in response.

My squeals sounded through the flat as Seb threw me over his shoulder and carried me to the bedroom where he dropped me in the middle of the bed.

"It's difficult to quantify the exact amount in words, so let me show you." Before the last word was out, Seb had pulled his t-shirt off over his head and his shorts and underwear were being pushed down together. His shoes clattered against whatever surface they hit, making me laugh again.

He reached forward and pulled my shoes from me before finding the button of my shorts that he made quick work of. My tiny lacy pants followed. I tugged my own vest off, but Seb intervened to remove my bra, taking the opportunity to draw each of my nipples into his mouth in turn, leaving them hard, aroused and aching.

"Fucking perfect, Princess."

He leaned back to admire his work then dropped to his knees at the side of the bed. With a hand on each of my ankles he pulled me down the bed until my legs hung off the end of it. Still holding them he placed my ankles on his shoulders and began to kiss his way down the length of my leg.

Slowly, he travelled down my left leg, pausing at my sex that was already opening for him to land a single kiss there. He travelled back up the right leg before making his way back down it. This time he kissed, licked, nibbled, and nipped at my flesh, paying extra attention to the thicker flesh of my inner thighs.

With a series of ouches that became low moans I relaxed into his touch, my most intimate folds softening and moistening more with every second that passed. The anticipation of what he might do once he came back to rest at the apex of my thighs was taking over my mind and body and when he did, it was even better than I'd anticipated.

The feel of Seb's tongue running along my length had me moaning and clutching the bed covers beneath me and he'd barely started. With his tongue going from licking my length to dipping into my core and circling my clit and back again, I was on the verge of coming apart. The addition of two fingers inside me, stroking and thrusting back and forth until I was calling to him, begging and pleading for release was a sublime form of torture.

"I really have missed you," he told me, his voice rumbling and vibrating across my clit that I was sure was swelling beneath Seb's tongue.

"I missed you, too." My words came out between a series of garbled breaths and gasps.

His fingers moved again, this time curling inside me, touching something deep inside me that had my body pulsing, but also gave me the sensation of needing a wee, however, it felt absolutely divine. Just as my release was about to break, Seb drew my clit into the wet heat of his mouth and I was screaming to him, pulling his hair and wrapping my legs around his head like I was an eastern European spy in a James Bond film.

I lay wrung out in a pool of sweat and tears when Seb

crawled up my body, kissing his way to my mouth where he shared the taste of me on his tongue.

"Told you I'd missed you." He grinned down at me as his erection nudged my opening.

"I thought you'd missed me more than that." My tease had the desired effect when he slammed into me.

"Maybe I did."

His lips crashed back to mine as his hips began to thrust fast and hard. I was moving up the bed under the force with which he was fucking me, and still I wanted more. My arms were around him and my nails clawed his shoulders and down his back, egging him on, pleading for more, and he didn't disappoint. His thrusts increased in power and speed until he was almost knocking the breath from my lungs. My head was bouncing off the headboard now and as his hands gripped my hips firmly, his fingers digging into the flesh there, I came, taking him with me in a series of grunts, hisses and sweat.

"You missed me that much?" I asked between gasps.

"More, but I might need ten minutes to show you exactly how much."

"I might need ten minutes to recover."

He laughed. "Thanks, glad to be of service."

I curled in against him and kissed his chest gently. "Always of service. I don't think anyone has ever missed me quite as much as you," I told him, and he pulled me in even closer and held me tightly.

"You'd better believe it."

"I really do miss you too, so much."

We stared at each other, both of us knowing that miss might just be becoming our safe word for love. The thought scared me, but I couldn't deny my feelings for him, however, I couldn't be the first to say it, just in case I'd read this wrong and my feelings were stronger than his.

He leaned in and kissed me gently. "I miss you enough that I'd like you to be my girlfriend."

I felt tears spring to my eyes, happy tears, the happiest I'd had.

"Yes," I managed before any tears were shed. "Boyfriend," I

said with a giggle.

"I might not need the full ten minutes for you, girlfriend," he told me as his lips met mine again and I found myself sprawled beneath him once more.

Chapter Nineteen

Seb

It had been a couple of weeks since Gabe returned from his honeymoon and today was the first time we'd done one of our lunchtime meet ups. I was relieved to be able to speak to him in private, just the two of us. No Bea and no Nanny. I might need to chat about me and Bea because things were good, great, and yet there were days when I got an uneasy feeling. Speaking of uneasy feelings, I needed to speak to my friend about his wife's threat to remove me from his and Charlotte's life if I pissed her off. I didn't think she meant it, but still…

I saw Gabe enter the café where we'd arranged to meet before he saw me, but as he looked around, he gave me a brief wave and a smile. Standing, I greeted him, genuinely pleased to see him.

"What a fucking week," he grumbled, taking his seat and reaching for the coffee I'd already ordered for him. "We need to do this again, with beer."

"Problem?" I asked, concerned for him suddenly.

"No, nothing major, just teething problems. Anyway, less about me and more about you, buddy. How are things with you and Bea?"

I grinned at the mention of her name and watched as he rolled his eyes.

"Fuck off. After all your doe-eyed expressions at Nanny before you bagged her, and since, if we're being honest, so, you have no room to judge me."

"Guilty as charged."

I smiled at his admission but spoke. "There's something going on with her. The family she works for. I told you they were splitting up?"

He nodded.

"But there's more. She's left and he is putting more and more on Bea, when he has to work late or go in early."

Gabe shrugged.

"Don't fucking shrug. He is their parent, not Bea."

"I know, but seriously, that's kind of her job, and before you jump in, I don't mean to parent the kids, but under the circumstances of a marital split and him being a senior professional."

I sighed and pushed my hand through my hair. "I know and I get that, but there's something I can't put my finger on, and Bea is sometimes off and it's not because of me. Plus, you never put on Nanny and she was there to care for Charlotte."

I looked across at him and my sense of victory was short lived, very.

"But I never wanted a nanny, and as such was determined that she wouldn't become my daughter's surrogate parent or someone who would essentially co-parent with me."

We both laughed loudly at the irony of his words.

"I know, I fucked that plan up in spectacular style. But I am sure Maurice isn't in the market for a new wife. He's barely rid of the last one."

"You think I'm worrying over nothing and imagining things that aren't there?"

He looked thoughtful. "Maybe, and maybe not. You know Bea better than I do and you would see her moods and changes in them far sooner than me, so there could be something there, but you might be worrying too much, too soon. What has Bea said?"

"That's the thing, nothing. She used to tell me about her work and funny things the kids said or did. She'd tell me what stuff was in their fridge that she'd never tried or seen or heard of, or even just what crap they fed the kids but now if I ask, she kind of shuts me down as soon as she can and changes the subject."

Gabe looked suspicious too.

"See."

"I do, and would be wondering what was going on too."

"Has she said anything to Nanny?"

His suspicion turned into awkwardness and discomfort now. "Don't do this. I don't want to be stuck in the middle or compromised. In the same way that I don't want to be involved when my wife asks me about what you've said about her friend, I don't want to be asked by my friend what my wife knows about his girlfriend."

"Sorry." I *was* sorry, but I was now sure that Nanny knew something I didn't, but as we were on the subject of Nanny... "Can I ask you something about Nanny then?"

Gabe stared across at me, hard. "If this question includes my wife naked, our honeymoon or anything risqué, I will punch you, hard."

I laughed, and as tempting as it was to make this a naked Nanny question, I didn't. "No, sadly not. When I joked about the gentleman's club, as well as threatening to cut my balls off she threatened me with you and Charlotte, or lack thereof to be more precise."

He nodded sadly and didn't seem surprised by me bringing it up. "And you want to know if she meant it?"

"I want to know if you'd let her do that." I was surprised by the annoyance in my tone.

"I guess as my wife and Charlotte's other parent she'd have some say and sway, but the truth is, she didn't mean it, not literally, but you'd have to majorly fuck up for me to support any attempt she might make in that endeavour. And by majorly fuck up I mean endanger life and limb, ours not your own."

"Thanks."

He shifted awkwardly in his seat. "We had some words about it. She shouldn't have said that to you, certainly not about Charlotte and I'm a big boy, I make my own decisions and choices. You're family, Seb, and nothing will change that, ever."

I nodded, feeling a little emotional at my best friend's words and the conviction with which he spoke.

"Maybe you and Carrie should have a conversation, just the

two of you…"

His voice trailed off and I knew exactly what he meant by talk. I offered him a very small and less than confident smile. I liked Nanny and respected her position as Gabe's wife and mother to Charlotte, but I was wary of us addressing that directly in case it got heated and she tried to assert her position and power over my friend and his daughter where I was concerned. By the same token, her reaction had been out of character so maybe I was worried about nothing.

"And you might want to have another conversation with Bea and discuss your concerns about her role in the household where she works."

"Fuck! When did you get so sensible?"

He wore his cocky and confident smile again. "When I hired a nanny, well, when I started shagging her."

I laughed loudly at his turn of phrase for the woman who was now his wife. Plus, he had been many things when he'd hired her and started shagging her, and none of them had been sensible.

He got exactly what had caused my laughter. "Okay, maybe once we got properly on track and I had the good sense to make her mine."

"Yeah. Bloody hell, if she exudes much more sensibility on you, I really will have to listen to you and take your advice."

He stared at me and flipped me off.

I grinned at him, happy to see his default flip off still there.

"Can we order some lunch? I am starving, I missed breakfast." He offered me his own grin. "Well, the sort served on a plate."

It was my turn to flip him off now, before we both scanned the menu.

Chapter Twenty

Bea

"And then what?" Carrie stared across at me, waiting for me to fill her in on all the details.

"Maybe I'm imagining things or just being melodramatic."

She looked doubtful. "Maybe, or maybe not. I don't know. What I do know is that Maurice is newly single, dumped no less, and by his own drunken admission, hasn't had sex for two years. He made a pass at you, one you rebuked and now, with his wife still AWOL and kids to care for he is passing that responsibility more and more onto you. So, what's next? I could be the one being melodramatic, but surely the lines will blur for him if you continue to take on more of Sophie's role. If you take on more of the mother role, how long before he views you that way, as the mother to his children, his wife?"

"Is that what happened with you and Gabe?" Once the words were out, they sounded a little hard and judgy and that is not how I'd meant them. Fortunately, Carrie didn't seem to take them that way.

She shrugged. "Possibly. I mean the lines blurred, for sure. I saw the father he was to Charlotte and I can't deny that my ovaries went pop on a regular basis and my lady parts loved that side of him, but that's not the issue with you and Maurice. It's the other way round for you and I do know that Gabe loved how I loved Charlotte. He eavesdropped on bedtime stories on the rare occasions he wasn't here to read them, and it was often after those moments with Charlotte that things got intense and heated."

I nodded, my friend made perfect sense, but she wanted Gabe as much as he wanted her. I didn't want Maurice as anything other than my boss. I mean, he was tall, dark, handsome and I could see the appeal of him, but not for me. Maybe if I'd been single I might feel differently. I didn't think I would though and maybe that was because I had only ever known and seen him up until this point as Mr Walker, my boss, Sophie's husband, Rosie and Craig's daddy, never as a man as it were.

"The fact that you are caring for his children, nurturing them, loving them, it could confuse him and in turn confuse his feelings for you."

I nodded. She made sense.

Carrie looked awkward and a little nervous as she appeared to be about to speak. I suspected what was on her mind and what she wanted to say.

"I'm not suggesting Maurice is a bad person and I do know that Toby was different, but..."

Her voice trailed off as she struggled to speak about her experience with our one-time friend who had drugged her, once for certain and possibly another time before. The second time he had tried to rape her and would have, had she not been rescued by Gabe and Seb. I shuddered at the memory and my own guilt for not airing my suspicions, not even that, just something I couldn't put my finger on sooner.

She reached across and grabbed my hand. "Anyway, that's in the past, but promise you'll be careful and not take any risks."

I nodded.

"Promise," she insisted.

I extended my hand and offered her my little finger. "Pinky promise," I said and grinned at my pinky promises with Seb and his theory on what happened if I broke another one.

Carrie grimaced at my little finger. "No chance! I know where your pinky promises have been." She shuddered with mock horror that made me laugh.

I withdrew my hand. "I promise."

"So, are we doing our girls night out on Saturday?"

I nodded, already excited by it. "Yup. Seb said him and Gabe were out Saturday, too. We could meet up with them at the end of the night if you wanted."

"Yeah, works for me, saves on us all having to get separate taxis and Gabe does love a drunken late-night reunion."

I laughed at her wiggling eyebrows. "I bet he does."

"Don't try and act so innocent. Can you honestly tell me that an alcohol fuelled Bea won't have Seb salivating at what debauchery he can incite from you?"

I threw the napkin I'd had next to me in her direction and flushed a deep crimson.

"I rest my case. Now, let's go and get the kids and maybe stop off at the park."

****

We'd taken the kids to the park and when Carrie had gone home with Charlotte, I'd brought the twins I cared for, Rosie and Craig, home.

After an afternoon snack we did some painting and reading before I began their evening meal which was my usual routine. As the pasta water came to the boil my phone alerted me to a message from Seb.

<Hey Princess, do you fancy dinner at mine tonight? I'll cook and you can tell me all about your date with Nanny. X >

<Would love to. Will let you know what time once I'm done here. You can tell me all about your date with Gabe. X>

<I can't divulge the details of guy time, not a date! You finish work at 5 so you don't need to let me know when you're done. X>

I stared down at the screen, unsure what to say. He was right. I worked seven til five as a rule, but that was when Sophie was home, she wasn't and Maurice seemed to be carrying on as if nothing had changed. I thought about what Carrie had said about blurred lines. I had nothing to say to Seb that would make a difference to his standpoint, so I made no reply. He had no such issue and his next message confirmed that.

<Just as I thought. I will pick you up from yours at 6. X>

Fortunately, Maurice arrived home at five on the dot. Unfortunately, after spending a little time with the children, he informed me that he needed to continue working from home and would be in his office if I needed him. I stared at his back as it disappeared down the hallway. *If I needed him?* I needed him to be a father to his children. Fuck! His children needed him to be their father as I was officially off the clock.

I followed him to his office and knocked the closed door. I heard noises behind it and waited. When he opened the door, he looked surprised to find me there.

"Yes."

I stared at him and finally seeming to sense that I might need a moment of his time, he moved back to his desk and invited me in. He pointed to the seat opposite him and I took it.

"I need to get off," I said and sounded nervous, not that I should have.

"If you could give me another hour, two tops—"

"Sorry," I interrupted him, certain he'd view it as some kind of insubordination on my part. "I need to go now. I finished over fifteen minutes ago."

He sat back in his seat and viewed me carefully, with interest. "I realise we're expecting more from you with things how they are. I need you, Bea."

The words hung there for a few seconds without either of us speaking.

"Me and the children," he added. "I'd appreciate your help and some flexibility while things are so uncertain. If you could give me an hour and then we could have dinner together and a drink, get to know each other—"

I cut him off again. "I have a date, a boyfriend. I have to go."

I leapt to my feet and without a glance back or a second thought I rushed out and ran all the way home with about ten minutes to spare before Seb would be arriving. I needed to calm down and push the evening's events from my mind. I needed to focus on Seb and our date for now, then tomorrow I would worry about my job and boss, assuming I still had either.

Chapter Twenty-One

Seb

It was Saturday night and while Bea was meeting Carrie in town, I was meeting Gabe at his. Bea had been a little under the weather the last couple of days, so I hoped she took it easy tonight. She'd made a joke about me trying to poison her after I'd cooked dinner for her the other night, which I wasn't, and whilst I didn't know what had made her unwell, she had definitely been under the weather.

I dressed casually in dark jeans and a white, button down shirt. Gabe and I were unlikely to make it a full-on bender tonight as we'd both got dates with our ladies later, plus, it now took a couple of days to recover from a heavy night. Maybe we really were getting too old for hard partying.

With my taxi waiting for me outside I headed out.

Gabe and Carrie were both still getting ready when I arrived and with their looks, touches and giggles I didn't need a diagram drawing of what had made them late.

I sat in the garden with a cold drink while I waited for Gabe to come downstairs, but it was Carrie who arrived first. She looked amazing in a white sundress that fitted to the waist and flared out to a fuller skirt that fell to just above her knees. She'd got white wedged sandals on her feet, her golden tan offset the white of her outfit perfectly. With her hair down and loose, she looked great.

"Is your husband likely to be much longer?"

She shrugged. "Who knows. He's trying a shirt on now."

We both laughed.

"Will you keep an eye on Bea for me, please?"

"Of course. Any particular reason why?" Nanny looked at me in a way that suggested she might just know the reason why.

"Just because she's been off for a few days."

She nodded, but something about the way she did made me suspicious. I had a niggling feeling that she knew something I didn't, and I really didn't like that.

"Have you spoke to her?"

Nanny shrugged and with that I knew she knew something. I didn't know why, I just did. "I saw her on Wednesday, and we've exchanged a couple of texts, but no more."

I was unsure whether to believe her or not and I didn't know why. My scrutiny of her was becoming more intense and she looked awkward at finding herself under it.

"Seb," she began, sounding a little nervous. "When you were here last…" her voice trailed off and I thought I knew where she was going with this. "I owe you an apology."

"I dunno about that but go on."

She sat on the small rattan stool next to the chair of a similar style and design I occupied. "I threatened to stop you seeing Gabe and Charlotte and I shouldn't have done that. I think we both know that I don't have that power or authority, but more than that, Gabe and Charlotte are your family in more ways than family often are."

"Thank you." I was genuinely touched that she had thought it through and realised she was wrong to have made the threat she had, whether she could carry it out or not. "And we are family too."

She cocked her head slightly, studying me and then she went on. "You weren't to know but you hit a nerve with the gentleman's club comment."

I laughed shortly, "I got that, Nanny, loud and clear."

She smiled across at me and looked embarrassed as she considered what to say next. "Gabe may have told you; I don't know. My mother, my birth mother was a prostitute."

I stared at her, agog. I was not expecting that. I shook my head. Gabe hadn't told me that.

"Well, safe to say my early years weren't the best. She drank and used drugs, too, and started off as, and I quote, a dancer."

"Fuck! I would never have said that to you had I even suspected. It really was a joke. I'm not saying Gabe and I have never been to some dodgy bars and strip joints, but not for years..." I had no clue what else to say so said nothing, simply allowing my voice to trail off.

"I really don't need to know about the dodgy joints you two have frequented." She pulled a pained expression and waved me away. "Not unless you want me to disinfect your bestie on a regular basis." She shuddered then gave a short laugh before turning serious again. "This information is not common knowledge, in fact, only you and Gabe know, and I'd like to keep it that way."

"Of course, it goes without saying," I reassured her.

"Right, I'm off to meet Bea. You need to keep my husband safe and relatively sober."

"Consider it done, Nanny." It felt as though we'd shared something that meant she liked me, independent of Gabe and trusted me, too. I really did like Nanny and was beginning to crave what she had with my friend. My mind wondered to Bea...and she was the one I might just be able to have it with.

Carrie got to her feet and turned to leave. At that second I wanted to repay her trust in me and share something with her, something very few others knew.

"Carrie." My use of her actual name seemed to startle her. "Gabe and I, and Charlotte...we are family. He was married to my sister."

Gabe appeared at that second and with a stunned expression, Nanny nodded at me with a sympathetic smile on her face.

"Angel, you're still here." Gabe grinned at her and leaned in to kiss her lips gently. "Waiting for just one last kiss?"

"Always, baby, always."

She pulled him close and hugged him, possibly because of the information I'd shared. Information Gabe clearly hadn't, surprising me slightly. She was now his wife and he had told her about the circumstances of my sister, his wife's death, although, I got that wasn't an easy conversation to have. It was seriously fucked up and painful, excruciatingly so, for us all.

Chapter Twenty-Two

Bea

"Why am I getting drunker than you?"

Carrie and I had matched each other drink for drink and yet I was beginning to get tipsy, unlike my friend who now shrugged. Maybe she had been putting some extra practice in on her honeymoon and her dinners for two with her new husband.

"Maybe we should get some shots in," I suggested.

"Not for me. Shots are not my friend, but I'll happily get more cocktails."

I nodded and watched her head to the bar. She looked amazing physically and every man in the place seemed to appreciate that, but for me it was more than that. She looked truly content and happy in her own skin and every time I saw her, she oozed more and more confidence.

When she returned from the bar we were on sex on the beach. She kept looking at me, suspiciously and why wouldn't she be? I had been deliberately evasive when she'd questioned me about how things were at work and if there was any news on Sophie or if Maurice had made any further advances towards me. I hadn't even told her about the weird exchange in his office a couple of nights before. I might have made more of that than there was and before Seb, if I'd been asked to work a little later, I would probably have done so without much in the way of a second thought.

My head was spinning with alcohol and thoughts and the pressure of them was making me frown, I could feel it forming and it appeared my friend hadn't missed it either.

"Bea, I'm worried about you." She stared across at me and the warmth in her eyes had me coming undone in a second.

"I'm worried about me." I could feel tears wanting to spring from my eyes.

"I'm not going to pry but if you want to talk."

I put my head in my hands and wondered where to start. "There's just so much going on right now, especially in my head."

Reaching across the table we sat at, she took my hand in hers, comforting and reassuring me.

"Right then, from the top. I dumped Seb before because I am totally in love with him and that was not part of our deal."

Carrie nodded, not surprised in the slightest.

"When we got back together, I told him, kind of, that I had feelings and he intimated as much in return. We haven't said it yet, but it feels like we're on the same page sometimes."

Again, my friend nodded, but did comment this time. "I loved Gabe from the first second I met him." She got a far-off expression as she thought about her husband. "I didn't like him though." She laughed. "But I fancied the pants off him. Speaking of which he still has a pair of my pants."

I stared, wide-eyed, unsure why he had her pants and whether he wore them or not. She didn't expand but returned to our conversation.

"I loved him before he loved me, well in terms of admitting it to ourselves. He was scared, more scared than me because of what he'd risked and lost in the past."

I assumed she meant him being a widower when they met, not that I knew any details beyond that. Carrie rarely referenced it and I had never heard Gabe or Seb say anything about the first Mrs Caldwell.

"Sometimes it just takes time and some circumstances to push for an acknowledgement, but I know Seb cares for you."

I nodded.

"Next," she called as if I had a list to get through, which I did, kind of.

I sighed, loudly and dropped my head to the table, then

explained about my weird encounter with my boss a couple of nights before.

"I told you the lines would blur, but fuck me, I wasn't expecting it so soon. I mean it was definitely a pass and if you were into him it could be sexy, but you're not, plus he sort of treated you like an old, worn pair of slippers rather than brand new designer heels."

I frowned at her analogy but got what she meant.

"What did Seb say?"

And there it was. I looked down and felt as guilty as I was sure I must have looked.

"Ah."

"Yeah, ah. I don't know if I should tell him or not. What would he even do or say? He'd probably laugh, especially if I reference me being old, worn slippers."

Carrie shook her head. "I don't think he would."

I shrugged, unsure what else to say.

"How was Maurice the following day?" She looked concerned for me now, worried that my boss might have continued with his unwelcome advances.

"Nothing. He acted completely normal and was very polite, but professional.

"Ah, okay. Maybe he figured he'd made a fool of himself and has put it behind him."

"I bloody hope so because I am constantly walking on eggshells."

"You should tell Seb though. Secrets have a habit of biting you on the arse when you least expect them to."

I nodded but neither of us were convinced that I would take her advice.

"Right, let's try the pornstar martini then." She got to her feet but before moving away, she smacked my arm quite firmly. "And you were supposed to tell me if he tried it on or if anything else happened. You promised."

She was definitely telling me off and I felt a little like a child in her care.

"Sorry." My one word was all I had to offer.

She frowned for a few seconds. "Hmmm. Right, pornstars

coming up."

I watched my friend head to the bar where the man serving her laughed at something she said as he took her order. Maybe I should have told her to bring them in twos because I had a feeling I was going to need more to drink before this night was out.

****

A couple more drinks later and with Carrie suggesting another toilet trip, I followed her to the bathroom. Once in there she jigged around until she got into the cubicle. I giggled from the neighbouring toilet and we chatted over the partitioning wall. She was out and washing her hands before me as I seemed to have some difficulty in pulling my own underwear up. Standing next to her at the sink I looked at our reflections. My make-up was beginning to smudge a little and my hair was dropping from the curls I'd put it into. Carrie on the other hand, still looked incredibly well put together. Her face looked fresh, although she was sporting her honeymoon tan still, so required very little in the way of make-up and her hair looked shiny and healthy.

She ruffled her locks and added a clear lip gloss. The effects of the alcohol sabotaged my own attempts to do anything to aid my appearance. Carrie laughed as I ended up with a smudge of lipstick on my face.

"Come here." She grabbed some tissue and cleaned me up before adjusting my hair. "How about we get a pitcher of an alcohol free one. It's quite refreshing…" Her voice trailed off when she realised she had just revealed her knowledge of alcohol free.

"That is why I am pissed, and you're still perfectly put together," I accused.

She grimaced apologetically. "I'm doing a dry night tonight."

"You could have said." I was a bit irritated that she'd pretended to be drinking drink for drink with me all night.

"I couldn't, wasn't supposed to…fuck it. I'm pregnant." Her grin almost split her face in half. "Early days, but that's why. Only Gabe and I know. It wasn't planned as such, but I was off the pill and we thought we'd see what happened and it seems no contraception, a honeymoon with a man I can't get enough of

93

means a baby is what happens."

I hugged her tightly unsure that I had ever been so happy for another person before. "How's Gabe taking it?"

She laughed. "He is beyond protective now, more so, but is absolutely thrilled. We haven't told Charlotte yet, as I say, early days, but once we know everything is good, we'll tell her then, so it's our secret for now."

I nodded and pulled her in for another hug and kept her there until another couple of women came in. "Come on then, show me the way of alcohol free."

Chapter Twenty-Three

Seb

The pace of things tonight was steady and relaxed. Neither Gabe nor I had any need to get drunk as lords or to make fools of ourselves, especially not as we were meeting up with the girls later. We had always been very similar in that we considered ourselves the alpha in a relationship, and as such we took care of our girl, so if they were likely to be drunk, which was a distinct possibility, then we needed to be sober and capable enough to care for them and keep them safe.

We were in a bar and sharing some banter when two women approached us, pretty women who were quite clear in their desire to get to know us better and to hook up.

"Hey," one smiled as they took seats opposite us.

Gabe shot me a glance that said this was a non-starter for him. It was a non-starter for me too, but I got where he was coming from because in the past, I would definitely have been up for it, with either or both of them.

"Nice to meet you ladies but we're both attached," I said, but they didn't look unduly concerned by that.

"We're not, and we won't tell," said the other one.

I laughed, couldn't help it. They were exactly the type of girls, women even, I could have had a very good night with, but not anymore. That realisation stemmed my laughter. I liked Bea and was getting sucked in deeper and deeper with every passing day.

Gabe glared at my laughter then turned to the ladies opposite us. "There'll be nothing to tell, ladies. I'm very happily married. A newly wed." He held his left hand up, showing them his wedding ring whilst wearing his happily, smug in love face.

They turned to me. "Not married, but very much happily attached."

They got to their feet and smiled.

"Have a good night and tell your ladies how lucky they are."

They walked away together while Gabe and I laughed.

"You're very much happily attached, are you?" Gabe asked with a wide grin.

"So it would seem."

He laughed at my reply and grimaced.

"You being very happily married was less of a shock."

"And I make no apology for it." His smug 'I'm in love' face intensified.

"Quite right too. I told Nanny about us being brothers-in-law."

Gabe had been lifting his glass to his lips. My final announcement stopped him mid lift.

"I see."

"I thought you may have already told her."

My friend shook his head. "Not my story, buddy."

"She told me about her mother."

"Again, not my story."

"I'm glad you met her and are sickeningly happy."

He laughed. "Well, it's about to get a whole lot more sickeningly happy." His face was at risk of splitting. "And this is absolutely my story. Carrie is pregnant."

It wasn't a surprise that they were going to have a child, but I hadn't expected it so soon.

"Fuck!" I muttered.

"Are you okay?" my friend asked, clearly startled by my reaction. "Most people would expect you to say congratulations, but I can see it's a shock." He laughed at me now.

"Sorry. Yes, congratulations." I pulled him in for a hug and a back slap before laughing. "I dread to think what Nanny will be like on hormones."

He laughed louder than me. "Horny, almost constantly, and

when she's not horny, she's hungry."

"Sounds perfect."

He scowled at me. "Do not think of my wife horny or getting pregnant," he warned.

I chuckled but couldn't deny I had indeed been thinking of Nanny in horny, shagging terms. "Come on, let's go and find the girls."

My friend nodded then downed the remnants of his drink. "This is highly classified information."

"My lips are sealed. Keeping mum, as it were."

****

The music was thumping and banging around the bar as we entered it. Bea and Carrie were easy to spot, dancing.

I turned to Gabe, to point them out, only to find that the sight of his wife in a white sundress and white underwear that was clearly visible due to the disco lights, had already caught his attention. His and almost every other man's in the place. I did nothing to hide or disguise my laughter as I gave him a dig in the ribs. He gave me one of our customary flip offs, before going to his wife, to retrieve her I imagined, but she had other ideas.

By the time I reached Bea and had pulled her into my arms, Gabe was being held and serenaded by Nanny. He had given up the fight against it and was a willing participant in their dance and I couldn't remember the last time I'd seen him looking quite so happy.

I left them to their dance and turned my attention to my own dance partner.

I kissed her cheek and whispered a single word. "Princess."

She completely softened into my hold and it was the best feeling in the world.

"Are you drunk?" I asked and thought she might be tipsy at least judging by her glazed expression and the number of times she'd stepped on my toes.

"A little. I tried alcohol free cocktails but they're not the same."

I laughed at her aghast expression.

"Of course they're not. I mean, just why?"

She nodded furiously. "Exactly."

"Do you want another drink?"

She shook her head. "Best not. I'm hoping for a very hot date when I get home."

"Are you indeed? How hot?" This girl never failed to amaze and thrill me with her open honesty.

"Scorching."

She bit into her lip and furrowed her brow nervously.

I pulled her even closer, she really was fucking adorable. "Scorching I can do, for you."

Gabe and Nanny suddenly appeared next to us, hand in hand.

"We're making a move," Gabe explained.

I nodded and looked at Carrie. "You feeling hungry, Nanny?"

She looked confused, unlike her husband who picked up on his earlier hungry or horny comment. We passed a very brief glance, but it was enough for her to pick up on it.

"You told him," she accused her husband. "About my increase in appetite." She wiggled her eyebrows and flushed.

I leaned in and kissed her on the cheek. "Congratulations, Nanny." I stopped and cocked my head with a sudden thought. "Am I going to have to rename you, Mummy."

She laughed, as did Bea, while Gabe sounded out a determined, "No! Fuck no!"

With that we all exchanged our goodnights, he took his wife home and I prepared to give my princess her scorching hot night.

Chapter Twenty-Four

Bea

"You are a bad influence, a very bad influence." I clutched my head, it was throbbing and aching like I didn't know was possible.

Seb looked across the table at me and laughed, loudly, too loudly.

"And that is not helping."

He shrugged at my final comment. "You were the one who suggested doing shots once we got back here."

"Why did you let me though?" I whined, looking for someone to blame for this hideous hangover.

"Because I am incapable of telling you no. Our scorching night will bear testament to that."

"Yeah, but scorching hot sex was good for me...shots were not."

He laughed again. "You want me to help you through your hangover?"

I squinted at him suspiciously. "Is that more sex you're offering? I might not be capable of being shaken or bent over without vomiting and you might need to keep the handcuffs out of things this morning." I looked at the clock. "Afternoon."

With wide eyes, Seb laughed. "I was thinking orange juice and a bacon sandwich followed by some pain killers...sex wasn't on offer."

I watched him, looking for some sign that he was winding me up, about there being no offer of sex. There were none. Shit!

Even hanging out of my arse I was all for shagging again, albeit minus the handcuffs. God, being handcuffed by my gorgeous boyfriend had been seriously hot. I had asked for scorching and by fuck, my man had delivered.

"Whatever," I muttered.

"Although, you looked seriously fucking sexy cuffed to the bed."

I was hot and achy again, remembering the feeling of being held down, captive, incapable of preventing him from doing anything he wanted. Fuck! As hungover as I was, my body was warming to the idea of more sex. Maybe we should do it again, sober, or at least without shots. The thought of those tiny little bombs of alcoholic destruction saw another wave of nausea wash over me.

"I'm going for a shower, but juice, bacon and tablets would be most welcome."

"Would you like me to scrub your back?" he called after me as I made my best effort to saunter away in my current, delicate state.

"Not unless you want me to vomit in the shower."

He said no more, but he did chuckle to himself.

****

Fortunately, I was hangover recovered by the time the working week started again. Maurice was his old self and I was inclined to agree with Carrie that he must have felt foolish after his clumsy pass and I was more than happy to pretend it had ever happened.

I was on my way to meet Carrie at the park with the kids when my phone rang, my mum. We weren't exactly close. We'd never fallen out, but were very different people and clashed, a lot. I answered the call and regretted it almost as soon as I did so.

The call was brief and to the point. My grandmother who I hadn't been close to either, had died. My mum thought I should know, and unsure what to say or how to react I had asked her to let me know when she had funeral details.

As if the call had never happened, I was getting good at ignoring things, I rounded the kids up and off we went with a picnic for lunch.

Carrie and Charlotte were already on the swings when we arrived. The kids all ran off together while my friend and I set out our blankets once I'd returned from the café with hot drinks.

"How are things?" she asked me.

I had no idea if things related to anything in particular or if she meant in general. To be certain I gave her details on everything.

"Maurice is his old self, Seb and I did shots when we got home on Saturday and had an amazing night. I paid for the shots on Sunday with the hangover from hell and I have received a call from my mother who tells me my grandmother has died."

"Wow! That's quite a weekend. I am sorry about your grandmother. Are you okay?"

I waved her condolences away as they weren't necessary, and I was absolutely fine. I explained as much.

"Honestly though, I am more interested in your amazing night."

We both giggled.

"I apologised to Seb about what I said about stopping him seeing Gabe and Charlotte."

I nodded. "He mentioned it."

"Did he mention anything else?" Carrie looked nervous.

I shook my head. "Like what?" Her question seemed anything but casual. There was something specific her and Seb had clearly discussed or knew of and she was fishing to see if I knew.

"We talked about our families and I just wondered if he'd mentioned anything."

I knew little about Carrie's family and possibly less about Seb's I realised at that moment.

"He didn't mention it at all."

She looked relieved. "So, just how amazing was your night."

We both giggled again as we lay back on our blankets and were joined by the children who all seemed to suddenly be starving.

With the picnic set up and us all tucking in, I looked across at Carrie. She sat cross legged and Charlotte, cross legged, sat within her mum's lap. They both looked happy, content and glowing, although they were both sporting nice tans so that might have been why they glowed, and in Carrie's case her pregnancy.

With a sandwich in one hand, Carrie's other hand stroked Charlotte's head with love and devotion oozing from her. Charlotte said something and as she turned slightly to look up at my friend, they both laugh. Without reservation and in an entirely natural gesture, Carrie leaned down and kissed the little girl's nose, resulting in even more laughter from them.

Unbeknownst to them, I watched for a couple more minutes, whilst chatting with the children in my care who I was very fond of, but by the time the children all went off to play again I had come to a realisation, a very big one. I wanted what Carrie had. I wanted to be happy, content and glowing with a baby growing inside me, the baby of a man I adored and who adored me in return, but for me that man wasn't Gabe, it was Seb.

And there it hit me. I loved Seb.

Chapter Twenty-Five

Seb

Bea was still acting weird at times. She did seem more settled generally, and yet I kept getting the feeling she was holding something back, as if she wanted to say something, tell me something, but wasn't.

I had just finished telling Gabe as much, having even gone so far as to tell him that we'd had a little fun with handcuffs, not that I gave him exact details, but I was fearful that she might be freaking out about that in the cold light of day.

"I assume she liked it at the time?" Gabe looked awkward as he asked the question I'd gone over in my head a dozen times or more.

"Yes, definitely." I couldn't keep the grin off my face as I recalled just how hot it was and how much she'd obviously enjoyed it. "It was fucking amazing, actually."

He shook his head but laughed with me. "How drunk was she?"

I stopped myself from bristling at him because I knew why he was asking.

"We did shots when we got home."

"Sounds messy."

"Her hangover was messier."

He laughed and then reminded me about the time Carrie threw up after he'd kissed her when she was drunk.

"Yeah, well she wasn't that drunk," I told him and continued. "She was drunk, we both were, but we were capable of making the choice to do that. She was capable of consenting."

"It never crossed my mind that you'd have done it without her permission." There was no doubt in his tone and I was in no way suspicious that there was any kind of inference in his words.

"And as I say, it was amazing. She was cool about it the next morning too."

"Doesn't sound like sober regrets or embarrassment then."

"No, that's what I thought."

"Seb." My friend looked at me, concerned. "Do you think she's having second thoughts? I mean she did kind of dump you before with no warning or explanation."

I closed my eyes and gathered my thoughts. He got me, knew me, and this is what I also kept coming back to. Was this Bea building up to dumping me again and because of how she'd done it last time, was she trying to give me the benefit of at least telling me first this time?

"I don't think so. We're happy. But then I was fucking clueless last time, wasn't I?"

He shrugged and checked his watch. "Ask her then, but it could just be that her grandmother has died, and she has to go back home for the funeral in a couple of days."

"Yeah. They weren't close, but she was still her gran, right?"

"Exactly," my friend agreed. "Look, I hate to run out on you, but Carrie has a doctor's appointment and as I insisted on going with her for it, the least I can do is be on time."

"Of course, go. Is Nanny okay?" I was suddenly concerned for her but felt certain she must be okay, or Gabe wouldn't have been so calm.

"Yeah, routine, pregnant stuff. Come for dinner, while Bea is away, unless you're going with her."

I shook my head. "I'd love to. She said she'd rather do it herself."

"Okay. Text Carrie and sort a day out. I really have to go." Like that, he was on his feet and heading for the door.

****

By the time I got home, Bea was just turning the corner and approaching my front door.

"Hi, babe," she called as she reached me, a broad smile

spread across her face.

She didn't look like someone who was ready to dump me. I pulled her in for a hug and dropped my lips to hers. "Hello, Princess. How was your day?"

"Good," she replied. "And it's not the best circumstances but I now have a long weekend off between my gran's funeral and Sophie coming home."

"How are things there?" I led Bea to the front door and wondered how Sophie and Maurice planned on making their situation right for their kids and for Bea because she didn't deserve to be stuck in the middle of their battle, and God knows the kids didn't deserve to be there.

Briefly, my mind wondered to a dark place in my past but the sensation of Bea pulling me closer as her lips moved against mine had me refocusing on her and the present.

"I missed you. A lot."

I smiled against her lips.

"So much that you need to fuck me, now," she told me more than asked and I couldn't think of anything I wanted more than some special one on one time with her, especially if she was going away for a few days.

"Should we go indoors first?"

"Entirely up to you, but the now was my priority."

"God! Could you even be more perfect?" I took her indoors in something between a carry and a drag and before the door had fully shut, we were all over each other.

We kissed for long seconds, devouring one another, unable to get close enough. Our mouths and tongues worked together to drive ourselves and each other up into something of a frenzy.

I was considering whether we'd make it to bed or if I should simply get us as far as the sofa when she broke our kiss and there, in the hallway, dropped to her knees.

"I thought you wanted me to fuck you?" I asked as she reached for the waistband of my trousers and I did nothing to stop her.

"I did, I do, but surely you fucking my face counts."

I stared down at her, already rock hard and when she spoke like that, in such graphic terms and with such colourful language, well, it only made me even harder. The idea of her spending all day playing games, teaching young, innocent children, taking trips to the park, feeding the ducks and nurturing young minds and then turning into this vixen who sought and gave pleasure without apology was an aphrodisiac like I had never known before.

She already had my dick out and was gently palming it. She looked up at me and licked her lips, her eyes full of desire and mischief. She gently fisted me a couple of times and then, with more pressure, she repeated it before licking the underneath of my length, paying special attention to that tiny piece of skin that seemed to join my dick to the gland. I hissed with pleasure as sensation ripped through me. The tiny curl of her lips begged me to throw her down and fuck her hard, but I wouldn't, not yet.

Slowly she consumed me, inch by inch, allowing her mouth, throat and gag reflex time to grow accustomed to my presence and then she began to move. Up and down from base to tip, circling her tongue around the head, then back down she went, over and over, cupping and caressing my balls at the same time until I couldn't think straight. Her speed picked up with each repetition and my hips began to thrust in time with her. I was close and getting closer.

"Princess," I warned her, but she didn't care. Her fingers squeezed the flesh of my behind that she cupped, it confirmed her intention to see me come undone from her position on her knees.

I reached down and grabbed her head and handfuls of her hair, tugging the strands as I moved with her until the tightening of my balls told me this was about to end. And end it did, in spectacular style. I came hard, Bea milking me as I struggled to remain standing, or see or think. I had never come so hard in my life. So hard it was almost painful. I swear my toes curled and I became double jointed as my body contorted in pleasure.

Eventually, my release ended and I came back down to the ground. I reached down and pulled Bea to her feet.

"Fucking hell, you need to meet me here every night if this is the standard of your welcome home."

She giggled and flushed slightly.

"I seriously owe you, now. So, food, a drink and then we should run a bath and spend the night with me between your spread thighs."

She laughed, probably at my less than romantic final comment, but seriously, I had no other plan. This girl was one of a kind and she was mine. That final thought terrified and thrilled me at the same time.

Chapter Twenty-Six

Bea

I was on edge, nervous and that was just at the thought of going back home for my grandmother's funeral. I was staying for a couple of nights at a local pub that offered bed and breakfast. Having a little distance would be in everyone's best interests, not that my family had offered me a bed.

My wardrobe mainly consisted of work clothes and going out clothes, not funeral clothes so I was popping over to check out Carrie's wardrobe and if she hadn't got anything suitable, we were going shopping to buy something that was.

Seb and Gabe were going to the gym together, having opted out of a group shopping trip, so when I got to my friend's house it was just me, her and Charlotte.

After a cup of tea, all three of us headed upstairs to Carrie's wardrobe. We were slightly different shapes, but Carrie felt certain she might have something that would fit and be suitable. To be honest, since her engagement to Gabe, she had enough clothes to open her own shop, not that she craved them, but Gabe loved to provide for her and spoil her, so I was certain we'd find something. She pulled a few dark coloured dresses out, then a couple of blouses and a skirt. She even threw a few pairs of shoes and boots my way.

"You don't need to borrow anything you don't like, but it seems silly to spend money on something you won't wear again."

I nodded and reached for the first dress. I stripped down to my underwear and slipped the dress over my head. It was a plain black shift dress but didn't quite fit right; too short, too tight across the chest with sleeves that looked as though someone had angered The Incredible Hulk.

Carrie and Charlotte both laughed at me.

"That's a no then."

I moved onto the skirt and a blouse.

"I look like I've got an interview. And the next."

I put on another dress, a slightly less formal one and it was perfect, finishing at the knee with three-quarter length sleeves that was flattering and respectful of the occasion. Just one problem, Carrie couldn't get the zip past my chest.

"I don't suppose you have it in a bigger size, do you?"

She laughed. "As this is my wardrobe and not a boutique, no."

"Worth a try." I took it off and checked the label so if I ended up shopping for something, I would start there.

Twenty minutes later and I had exhausted all the possibilities of Carrie's wardrobe. Charlotte was clip clopping around in her mummy's shoes, a very high and sparkly pair. I dropped onto the bed next to my friend and pouted.

"If only your boobs were a bit bigger...that dress would have fitted me then."

She laughed. "Sorry. Although that dress was always baggy around the chest. It's only that my boobs have exploded—" she pointed down at her pretty flat looking tummy. "—that it's tight on me."

I stared across at her, absorbed her words then leapt to my feet. "Come on, we need to go shopping."

I turned and headed for the stairs while my friend called after me, confused at my hurry.

"Charlotte, let's go shopping to buy pretty things," I shouted over my shoulder to the little girl and almost immediately heard the clatter of Carrie's shoes bouncing off something hard.

****

Once we got to the shops Charlotte needed a wee, a drink, another wee and something to eat meaning that after an hour I was no closer to buying anything.

Carrie watched me as she sipped her bottled water while Charlotte sat chatting to a little girl on the next table.

"What?" I snapped, uncomfortable and agitated to find myself under her studious gaze.

"I could ask the same. I get you liked the dress, but you didn't seem unduly upset until I said it was bigger across the chest."

"Fuck, fuck, fuck," I hissed, dropping my head to the table, hard and loud. Loud enough that it drew the gazes of people nearby.

I felt Carrie's hands on each side of my head and as she lifted it, I realised she was crouched at my side, looking at me again, concerned.

"I need to buy a dress and a pregnancy test."

She almost fell back on her arse at that revelation. "Fuck, fuck, fuck, indeed." Once safely back on her chair she struggled to look at me, then asked, "Is it Seb's, if you are, I mean?"

I was unsure if I should have been insulted by her question that more than inferred I could be carrying anyone else's baby. Seb and I had been back together a couple of months now and exclusive so there was no way, if I was pregnant that it could be anyone else's. Instead of getting mad at my friend, who I knew would support me regardless, I nodded.

"Does he know, have you mentioned it?"

I shook my head, thinking how ridiculous I was not to have suspected before myself. "It was when you said about the dress and your boobs, because, you know." I pointed towards her tummy. "And I need you not to tell him or Gabe."

"I won't lie to Gabe, but I don't imagine he will ask if you're pregnant so we should be safe." She offered a small smile.

"Thanks. And in the event that he does ask if I'm pregnant, you can just laugh, hysterically, not that there is anything amusing in this hideous situation."

She nodded and then turned practical. "Why do you think you might be?"

"Because I haven't had a period since we got back together, and I might have been a bit off the last few days."

"Charlotte, sweetie, let's go, we need to shop for Bea. Say bye-bye to your new friend," she told the little girl.

I found a dress, similar to Carrie's that I hadn't been able to fit my boobs into. I sat in my bedroom, hung the dress on the wardrobe door, pretended I may not be pregnant and refused to do the test until the morning. It said you could take the test any time of the day, but I had already decided to wait until the following day, partly because any hormones would be more concentrated then, and a bigger part because I was shit scared to be faced with the reality of finding myself pregnant with the baby of a man I was barely past being fuck buddies with.

Chapter Twenty-Seven

Seb

Waking, I realised I was alone in bed. Yesterday, Gabe and I had been to the gym while the girls ended up going shopping for something for Bea's grandmother's funeral. I had thought we were meeting up at Gabe's and then spending the evening together but when I got back to my friend's house she wasn't there. Nanny had explained that Bea had been a little out of sorts, possibly due to going back home and meeting up with her family. I wasn't convinced. When I called her, she was chatty and bright, too chatty and bright, leaving me more convinced that something was wrong. I'd suggested having dinner and spending the night together, but she'd blown me off and not in a good way.

I reached beneath the bed covers and rubbing my hand over my morning erection I thought back to her on her knees, blowing me off in the best way possible.

"Shit!" I needed to get my arse out of bed, showered and confront Bea because there was more to her weird moods and being out of sorts these last few weeks and I was determined to uncover what was behind it all.

****

I was as nervous as I'd ever been when I arrived at Bea's place. My palms sweated and there was a heavy knot in my stomach. Standing on the front steps I hit the intercom and without saying a word, the door was released.

My breathing was a little heavy once I reached the top of the building where I found Bea's door already opened for me. I entered and found her in the small kitchen, boiling a kettle.

"How's my princess?" I asked, already sidling up behind her, wrapping my arms around her middle and kissing her neck.

"Hoping to get the next few days over and done with."

"I understand that. Let me come with you, help you through it?"

She spun in my embrace and reached up to cup my face. "Thank you, but no. My family aren't bad people as such, but they're critical and negative and we're not close, so, I would rather do this on my own."

I nodded, reluctantly and took in Bea's face. She was beautiful but looked tired and tense. Her skin looked a little pale, but I wouldn't have gone as far as to say she was unwell. Maybe she was just stressed about going home, exactly as she'd kept telling me. Maybe it was me, overthinking it and making a drama where there wasn't one.

"What do you want to do today?"

She shrugged. "Maybe we could have a lazy afternoon in front of the TV, drinking tea and eating biscuits."

"Fuck! If that doesn't sound like the best way to spend an afternoon, I don't know what does...although, I can think of something that might improve that plan." I gave her a smirk and a wink that made her laugh.

She shook her head at me. "One-track mind you've got yourself there."

"And you love it." I leaned in and dropped a single, gentle kiss to her lips before reaching past her to grab the biscuit jar. "I will see you on the sofa warming the remote control up and I'll take regular tea, none of that fruity, herby shit you've been known to suffer."

"It has health and wellbeing benefits."

I laughed at her claims. "You are a sales departments dream. You believe everything they tell you, plus, who in their right mind would dunk their Hob-Nobs in a cup of lukewarm water infused with thistles, donkey anus and hibiscus, whatever the fuck that is."

She laughed loudly at my protests and shook her head.

"Hibiscus is a plant, a flower, and I do not consume donkey anus."

"Maybe not, but you would if an advertising campaign told you it would help your hair and nails to grow, and I dread to think what you'd allow to pass your lips with the dangling carrot of weight loss."

She stuck her tongue out at me. "I've never heard you complain when I've allowed you to pass my lips."

"I love passing your lips almost as much as you do."

She scowled, but rather than coming back at me she stared at me, a strange expression on her face as I backed off and watched her watching me. Yet again, I wasn't convinced that there wasn't something else going on with her, in fact, I would have put money on it.

We'd had tea and far too many biscuits on my part whilst watching an old action movie I'd fallen asleep in front of. I awoke to find myself alone. Looking around there was no sign of Bea. I prepared to get up and find her when I heard her.

The sounds from the bathroom weren't the most attractive, but my concern for Bea outweighed everything else. I tapped on the door and called her name gently. Her response sounded like vomiting followed by heaving.

"Bea," I called again. This time, I opened the door slowly and repeated the call of her name.

"No," she shouted, but was heaving and vomiting again and I had already entered the bathroom.

The scene before me was one of Bea kneeling to the front of the toilet, her head hanging down the bowl as whatever was left in her stomach was expelled. I approached her, pulled her hair back and gently stroked her back. This was not stress, it couldn't be, could it?

"Bea, Princess, is there anything I can do?"

She reached up, flushed the chain, shook her head and washed her face.

"Is it something you ate or—"

"No, not something I ate."

I looked at her as she sat down on the now closed toilet lid. "So, if it wasn't something you ate, maybe a bug off one of the kids—"

Again, she cut me off with a shake of her head, worrying me. Then what could it be?

"Seb." She reached across to where I sat on the side of the bath and took my hand in hers. "I'm pregnant."

The world stopped for long seconds. She was pregnant. She couldn't be. How? When? Fuck me! Never mind her being sick, I was going to be sick in a second. She looked at me expectantly, waiting for something from me.

"Is it mine?"

She glared at me. Clearly that's not what she'd expected, wanted or needed from me.

"Yes, it's fucking yours."

She angrily sprang to her feet.

"Who else's could it be?"

"Sorry." I was sorry for insulting her.

"Yeah, well, that's okay then!" she spat at me, angrier than ever.

I shook my head and sat in silence.

"Say something," she implored.

"No."

My single word response had confused her judging by her face.

"No. You can't be. We have never discussed this, never, so, no."

"But I am."

She looked as though she was about to cry, but this was too much. I couldn't do this.

"No," I repeated. "We can't have a baby. I do not want a baby."

I got to my feet, heaving in a deep breath and faced her. She looked scared.

"I'll leave you to think things through, and we'll speak when you come back from visiting your family."

And then I turned and left without a look back, although the sound of her cries haunted every step I took.

Chapter Twenty-Eight

Bea

I watched Seb's back disappear and felt my heart break a little more when the sobs and cries left my body, and what's worse, he didn't even glance back.

What was I going to do now? I was pregnant, in love with my baby's father and he, well, he couldn't even bear to be in the same room as me. He had walked out after questioning if the baby was even his, and that was before he told me that I couldn't be pregnant and realising I could, his mind was changed to him not wanting a baby. Well, that was tough shit because I was having this baby. Clearly alone, but I was having it nevertheless so, fuck him.

With a glass of water and a dry biscuit I made my way to the sofa and between bouts of crying, checked my phone. Hoping desperately for some contact or acknowledgement. There was none. I skimmed through social media and felt sick as every inspirational quote and meme seemed to relate to me and Seb.

"Fuck it!" I turned my phone off, showered, brushed my teeth and put on clean pyjamas before climbing into bed to watch movies.

I eye rolled until my eyes were at risk of getting lost in the back of my head at each and every kiss, cheesy line or too good to be true male that appeared on my screen.

My advice of, 'don't believe him,' and comments like, 'lying bastard' went largely unheeded by the women in the films who were as gullible as I had been. When would I learn? I hoped I had a daughter so I could raise her to trust nobody and to only have expectations of herself.

Carrie, my also pregnant friend, had asked me to let her know what the outcome of my pregnancy test had been, but as her husband was best friends with my lowlife baby daddy I was sure she'd know soon enough, plus, I didn't want to talk to anyone right now.

Anger was replacing my initial hurt at Seb's reaction. I didn't deserve this. Our baby didn't deserve this, but there was more. I hadn't got pregnant deliberately or alone and he needed to get his head out of his arse and accept some responsibility as I accepted mine. God, I wished I could get drunk. That thought made me feel guilty as I remembered getting drunk on my last night out with Carrie. I felt sick thinking that I might have damaged my baby.

I placed a hand over my flat stomach. "I promise to take care of you properly now that I know you're there." And I would, the best of care, but for now I needed to focus on not crying about this now. My eyes were sore, my nose snotty and my head ached, and that wasn't good for either of us.

Maybe Seb would think about things and make contact after sleeping on it, before I went home for my gran's funeral that was going to be even harder if he didn't.

****

The following morning, I had heard nothing from Seb when I turn my phone on to check. There was a message off Carrie asking whether she was going to have a pregnant pal. I didn't reply and turned my phone off again.

Once showered and dressed, I grabbed a small suitcase and packed enough for the next few days and folded my new dress to pack too. I had booked a train ticket that allowed me to use any off-peak train and with nothing keeping me at home, I headed to the station.

I foolishly kept looking for Seb, hoping he would pop up from somewhere and tell me that he'd been an idiot and that he loved me and was thrilled to be having a baby with me. I wanted him to beg for forgiveness and to tell me that I was the only girl for him and that he intended to make things up to me for the rest of our lives. He didn't do any of those things, and as my train pulled out of the station, I couldn't help but shed more tears for what we could have had and in turn what we'd lost, all of us, me, him and most of all, our baby.

The man next to me smiled but looked incredibly uncomfortable at my tears and upset. Truth be told, I was uncomfortable at my tears and upset.

I found the journey cathartic, gazing out of the window, watching the world go by, emptying my mind and thinking of nothing. I really needed to think of nothing right now, because otherwise all I could think about was being pregnant and alone, Seb and the reality of being a single parent in seven or eight month's time. I had no money or support. My home was a one bedroom flat in the attic. The thought of climbing those stairs, pregnant, with a baby or a pushchair were the things of nightmares, and yet I knew I couldn't afford anywhere bigger or better. How was I going to make rent payments on my current home, never mind afford a more suitable one? This was a big mess, no doubt about it, and yet I couldn't and wouldn't get rid of my own baby. He or she was mine, forever, and I was strong enough to get both of us through the hard times. One way or another I would do whatever it took.

When I arrived at my destination, I felt a familiarity at my surroundings. Nothing had changed since I'd left, nothing except me. I took the short walk from the station to the pub that sat in the middle of the village square. I checked in and was immediately recognised by the landlord whose daughter I had gone to school with. After a bit of a catch up he showed me to my room that overlooked the square where I'd spent hours of my youth. I smiled at the place if not all the memories. I unpacked and after a restless night the previous night, I lay down on the bed and fell into a deep sleep.

Chapter Twenty-Nine

Seb

I woke up with the hangover from hell, but unfortunately, I wasn't able to go back to bed and pretend the last twenty-four hours hadn't happened. Worse still was the fact that I was expected at Gabe and Carrie's. Under the circumstances the last thing I needed was to watch my newlywed friend and his pregnant wife play happy families with my niece.

Would I get away with cancelling or just not turning up? No, not a chance, especially not if Bea had told Carrie she was pregnant and that I had rejected her and run for the fucking hills. Maybe I should go and see her, but to what end? I wouldn't do this to myself, couldn't, so she was better off doing this on her own and deciding what she wanted for herself.

My head was still banging by the time I got to Gabe's. He greeted me with a smirk.

"Good night?" he asked.

Before he could answer, Carrie appeared and laughed at my delicate state. "Looks like someone had a fun night. It explains why Bea isn't taking my calls. Did she get off okay?"

I stared at her and was clueless what to say. I wanted to talk to Gabe, alone, but with her standing in front of me, I couldn't exactly ignore Carrie, especially not when she was looking at me expectantly. She knew something. If she didn't know Bea was pregnant, she suspected it. Fuck!

"I haven't seen her today."

Gabe and Carrie stared at me. The latter looked

disbelievingly, whilst the former knew something was up.

"Where's Charlotte?" I asked, hoping for a distraction.

"She's gone out with Mum and Dad. They've gone to visit Granny."

I smiled at the thought of Margaret, as I usually did.

Gabe moved his position so he was able to guide me into the lounge, but he hung back slightly, probably to indicate that Carrie shouldn't follow.

Once alone with my friend, I dropped to the sofa and let out the longest, loudest sigh I might ever have known.

"That bad?"

"And so much fucking worse."

"You want to talk?"

"I think I probably need to, but I can't see how any amount of talking is going to sort this mess out."

He nodded, clueless as to just how deep the shit I was currently in was.

"Bea was unwell yesterday, vomiting. I thought it was something she'd eaten or a bug or something. It wasn't."

He stared at me and I think, suspected the cause of my girlfriend's illness, or ex-girlfriend as it was.

"She's pregnant."

"Fucking hell!"

"Yeah."

"What happened?"

I freaked out. I told her she couldn't be after I asked if it was mine."

"That was a dick move, mate, the asking if it was yours."

I shrugged. I knew her baby was mine.

"So, where are things at now?"

"Fucked up beyond recognition. After I told her she couldn't be pregnant, I went on to tell her that we couldn't and that I wouldn't have a baby. I walked out to the sound of her crying without looking back then went home and got drunk beyond belief. I haven't heard from her or made contact." I risked looking up at my friend and although his face clearly conveyed that he thought my actions had been a mistake, he didn't look at me with anything resembling disapproval because he knew where I was coming from.

Before either of us said anything else, there was another voice, one that was full of disapproval.

"You bastard! You fucking bastard! What the fuck gives you the right to do that to any woman, especially Bea? She was shitting herself thinking that she might be in this position. She thought you may be shocked, upset...she was shocked and upset at the prospect of being pregnant. You have treated her like a glorified fuck buddy at times, but I thought you were better than this. I certainly thought you were better than dumping the woman you've fucking knocked up, and as for you walking out to the sound of her cries without a look back...I don't think I have ever been more disgusted in another human being as I am with you."

Carrie eventually took a breath, allowing Gabe a chance to address her. "Angel, this isn't as cut and dried as you think, and it really isn't any of your business."

She looked seriously pissed with her husband now, taking the heat off me, if only for a little while I assumed.

"Really? You think he has acted decently in this?"

Before Gabe could offer a response, she carried on.

"You should think very carefully before answering."

There was no mistaking the threat of consequences to her husband and his possible reply.

"You don't know what's happening here," he told her again.

"Don't I? And as for it being none of my business, she is my friend." I looked up at her strained voice and thought she might be ready to cry.

"I should go." I got to my feet.

"Yes, you should," Carrie spat.

"No, you shouldn't, park your arse," Gabe told me.

Carrie was seething. "She's my friend," she repeated. "What do you expect me to do?"

Gabe reached for his wife and gently stroked her cheek. "I know, but you don't understand, and while Bea is your friend, Seb is my family. Our family."

If looks could kill she would have buried me on the spot with the one she gave me, and that paled compared to the glare she shot her husband.

"Well, you know what they say, you can choose your friends —"

Gabe had clearly run out of patience with his wife and her utter contempt for me and determination to argue with him.

"For fuck's sake. This is not your business. I told you to give me and Seb some space, but instead you chose not to and maybe even did a little eavesdropping. You don't get to be the moral majority here. You. Do. Not. Know. All. The. Facts."

The last words were punctuated for maximum effect.

Carrie glared at Gabe as if she barely recognised him.

"If you think his—" she pointed at me— "behaviour is in any way acceptable then I don't know you at all. And whilst I don't know all the facts, I do know what it's like to be pregnant, even if you didn't tell me I couldn't be before abandoning me."

She turned away and with a huff followed by her first cry she left me and my friend alone again.

"Sorry," I told him.

"You need to sort this out, in your head. I won't be stuck between you and Carrie and I won't allow Charlotte to be either. The fact is that Bea is pregnant, buddy, whether you like it or not."

I nodded and buried my face in my hands whilst letting out a few growls and muttered curses before getting to my feet.

"Where are you going?" Gabe asked.

"To see your wife and fill the gaps for her."

"You don't need to do that. She's pissed off, but that doesn't mean you put her need for knowledge ahead of your need to keep it to yourself."

I stared at him and felt tears spring to my eyes. I headed for him and pulled him in for a huge hug.

"You are the best friend I could ever have asked for. Thank you. But I think I'd like Nanny to know, especially if she isn't going to hate me."

"And Bea."

"Not a fucking clue, mate, but you're right, she is pregnant, and I can't change that, and I certainly can't act like a dick and wish it away."

I turned away again, with Nanny as my only destination.

Chapter Thirty

Carrie

My mood had gone beyond fury, but I was unsure who I felt most pissed off with, Seb or Gabe. I couldn't believe the latter had the audacity to side with Seb and had essentially told me to butt out and shut the fuck up, while supporting his douchebag friend who had acted abhorrently in his treatment of Bea.

God, poor Bea. I unlocked my phone and prepared to send her a text, checking if she was okay, as okay as she could be, but also to let her know that I was going to be there to support her, regardless of Seb's involvement and behaviour or that of my husband.

Movement in the doorway caught my eye. I looked up and saw Seb standing there with Gabe behind him.

"Can I come in?" Seb asked.

I waved a hand around the kitchen. "It would appear that you can do no wrong so I am sure you can go wherever you want around here."

"Carrie," warned Gabe but that single use of my name only confirmed that I was more pissed off with him than his friend.

Moving to the table, I gestured for Seb to join me. "There is nothing you can say that will make me change my opinion of your actions towards Bea."

"Carrie," Gabe repeated, gaining my full attention.

"You do not get to reprimand me. I am not a child. I am an adult, your wife, your partner, your equal, or so I thought. You choose to support what Seb does? Then that is on you, but you do not get to make me submit to your opinions, ever."

Gabe said nothing but did push Seb into the room, taking a seat next to me, leaving Seb to take one opposite me.

"Go on then. Give it your best shot." This surely had to end badly because I was becoming more annoyed with every fucking second that passed and every word either of them spoke.

Seb looked sad, desperate and I couldn't get my head around that, especially not when he began to wring his hands and breathe deeply.

Gabe looked across at him and patted his shoulder supportively then told him, "You don't have to do this if you're not ready."

I glared at my husband but then looking at Seb again he looked broken as he opened his mouth to speak.

"You know about Alice?"

I nodded. "Charlotte's mother."

"Yeah, and you remember she was my sister?"

I nodded again.

"And you know what happened to Charlotte and Imogen?"

"The baby? Imogen?" I hadn't known her name until that second when he had uttered it on a heart wrenching sob.

"Yes, the baby. She was named Imogen because it meant beloved child. She'd been wanted so much."

I stared across at him and then glanced at Gabe who was holding his head in his hands.

"I told you Alice was my sister."

"Yes."

"She was. She was my adoptive sister. I grew up in care for a while and was lucky enough to be adopted."

It seemed that Seb and I had more in common than I'd known and I could certainly relate to the feeling of good fortune in being adopted but had no clue where this was going or how it related to Bea.

"My parents were lovely people. My dad was my mum's second husband. Her first husband, Alice's dad, had run off and never looked back. Alice and I grew up together as siblings and for the most part we got along. We had our fights and differences of opinion, like any brother and sister, but I never suspected anything was wrong with her...anyway, when she was about seventeen, she sought out her birth father."

I was still clueless where this was going but had no choice but to let this unfold. Looking down, I realised Gabe had taken my hand in his, and although still irked with him, a little of my anger had subsided, probably due to my confused state of mind and the fact that this trip down memory lane with Alice in the leading role must be hard for him.

"Did she find him?"

Seb nodded. "Yeah. He had grown up after leaving our mum and had met someone else. They'd had more children. He was happy and stable, and Alice set about rebuilding her relationship with him and his new family."

I frowned, my confusion due to what he was saying and how this related to Bea was escalating.

"Seb, I don't understand what this has to do with Bea being pregnant."

"You will. It was a couple of years later, Gabe and I were going to the same uni and then I discovered Alice had been accepted there too. What I didn't know at that stage was that her half-sister, Cheryl had also been accepted. We all went off to uni and met up at a party." He looked across at my husband and smiled. "Gabe and I met at secondary school, a boy's grammar school and he'd met Alice a few times, but it wasn't until this party that they got together."

I didn't look at Gabe for fear that he might be wearing a longing look for a past he'd shared with a woman who wasn't me. Maybe this was down to hormones because the mention of Alice was pissing me off, after what she did...

"We all met up fairly regularly. Cheryl and I hit it off like you wouldn't believe. When Alice and Gabe got together, I wasn't exactly thrilled because I knew Gabe wanted love, marriage, a family and that had never been something I imagined Alice wanting."

He smiled sadly and my heart sank.

"Cheryl and I dated, got married, had a baby, like Gabe and Alice."

I was agog, and Seb was hysterical. The sound and sight of

him howling, like an animal, scared and in pain, took me back completely. I stared at the heartbroken man before me and knew what he was telling me.

"Oh God, Seb." I felt tears making my own face wet and I sobbed and shook at his grief and the horror of the actual reality of it.

Gabe released my hand after stroking my knuckles then moved to comfort his friend before picking up the story.

"Seb and I have been best friends since school. My wife was his sister, but also his sister-in-law, he is Charlotte's uncle, but he was also Imogen's father."

I got to my feet, unsure what to do. Unsure if I was capable of standing, never mind moving. My head was awash with emotions and although I would never agree that his treatment of Bea was anything other than wrong, I could understand his reluctance to become a father again. I remembered Gabe's guilt about Alice, her past that had been uncovered and that he had never suspected anything, although I now knew that there would have been guilt for the pain Seb had endured. With that in mind I could only imagine the guilt, albeit unwarranted, that Seb must have felt and still felt at not preventing his daughter's death.

Seb still sobbed and Gabe essentially held him, something he allowed him to do. I looked at my husband who had just shed the first of his own tears. Unable to do anything else I joined them and although my arms were considerably shorter than theirs, I wrapped an arm around each of them and hoped I would never know the pain either of them had.

Chapter Thirty-One

Gabe

I stood, in my own kitchen holding my friend close, almost rocking him as he cried. It wasn't the first time I'd done this for him, but it was the first time we'd done it with an audience, albeit an audience of one. My wife cried silently as she watched my friend's distress and offered me a small smile, although that friendly gesture in no way fooled me into thinking that she wasn't still pissed with me despite the fact she'd joined us and held us both until a short time before.

Seconds turned into minutes and finally, Seb quieted.

"Sorry." He attempted to get to his feet, but Carrie was on hers before him.

"There is nothing to apologise for. I can't imagine the pain you've endured. Let me get some food and drink sorted. We can eat outdoors if you want to?"

"Are you sure? I can go—"

"Seb." She cut him off. "You're going nowhere right now. We'll eat and then you need to decide what you're going to do about Bea."

I interjected. "Angel—"

It was me who was cut off now. "You don't get to tell me I'm not allowed to speak, to express my opinion."

Yes, she was pissed at me and when my friend did go, I was going to cop it.

She turned to Seb again. "You don't have to discuss it with me, but for yourself, you need to think long and hard about what you want, and then you need to do right by Bea."

Seb nodded. "I know she's your friend."

Carrie frowned at him. "Nothing to do with it. She is a human being and you, well, you can be a bit of a dickhead, but you are good and kind and would never forgive yourself if you just walked away from all of this, like this."

He nodded again.

I watched on and for all that Seb and I were the professionals here, well, my wife was knocking it out of the park with her ability to get straight to the heart of the matter, calmly and concisely. The way she tapped into my friend's goodness and kindness as well as his need to do right was a sight to behold.

She stretched up and stroked my friend's cheek before pulling him down to kiss his other cheek. "I love you, Seb, even when you're a dickhead, but there's a line."

She turned and headed into the kitchen, leaving me and Seb staring between my wife and each other.

We did eat together outdoors and although we chatted, nobody mentioned Bea or her pregnancy, although I suspected my wife had text her.

Shortly after the slam of a car door, Charlotte and my parents appeared in the garden. Charlotte kissed us all and after climbing on Seb's lap told us about her visit to Granny. My parents left almost immediately, citing a date night, which I didn't need to think of and once Seb had caught up on Charlotte's week she went off to play on the trampoline.

It was at that point that Seb addressed the elephant in the room. "I will call Bea, speak to her, properly. I can't say I saw this coming and it's a huge shock, but that's no excuse for the way I behaved, I know that."

"Good." Carrie smiled as she uttered the single word. "And it was a shock for her too."

Seb nodded. "It never occurred to me that she had entrapped me in any way, but it was a shock," he repeated. "And when I asked if it was mine, I didn't doubt it was, not really."

Carrie nodded and then shocked me and Seb when she said, "I asked her the same and I never expected any reply other than yes, not that she knew she was at that point."

"It makes sense now, all the strange moods and being off about stuff."

"I can certainly relate to that," I said making my friend laugh, my wife, not so much so.

"Really? Did you actually say that in front of me? And if you think my moods have been strange up to this point, you ain't seen nothing yet."

I was unsure if my wife was making a threat or a promise. She turned back to Seb.

"Yeah and with work being as it is, well, her moods have been all over the place."

He nodded. My wife continued.

"Hopefully, once Maurice and Sophie sort their shit out it should be better and more settled, and she needs stability. Plus, now that he's not blurring the lines between her being his children's nanny and his wife—"

She actually interrupted herself with a gasp and a horrified expression.

"What the fuck does that mean?" Seb spoke quietly and flatly but there was no mistaking the annoyed glint in his eye and the muscle in his cheek twitching.

"I didn't mean to say that, and I thought she may have told you and you knew work had affected her moods." Carrie was offering a defence but without adding any details, annoying Seb further.

He glared across at her, which even if I did understand the cause of his annoyance, I wasn't about to let him speak to her this way, especially not in her own home.

"Seb, friends talk, like we talk, and this is not Carrie's fault, none of it so think carefully before you proceed with speaking to my wife."

He took a deep breath. "Nanny, please."

Carrie sighed, but with no real other choice went on to explain that Bea's boss had tried it on with her. He hadn't made any overtly physical moves but had made it clear he'd be up for sex and had made more than one comment that invited Bea to spend some time alone with him. The time he'd made a clear pass had been when he had come home drunk and was incapable of taking care of his own children.

Seb looked far from happy at these revelations, and I didn't blame him for that, but at least him and Carrie had made up and he did seem more settled now.

"What will you do, about Bea and the baby?" Carrie asked.

"Angel," I said, thinking it was unlikely Seb would have a real response to that.

She glared at me. Yup, I was still in the doghouse, then she turned her attention to my friend once more.

"I can't change the fact that she's pregnant, so I'll have to accept it and support whatever decision Bea makes, beyond that I don't know what I'll do."

Carrie shook her head and with four words asked the question we all wanted to know the answer to, not that I was sure even Seb knew what that was. "What do you want?"

Chapter Thirty-Two

Bea

Standing at my gran's grave, the tears ran down my face and I was unable to slow them never mind stop them. The saddest thing was that the tears were not for my deceased grandparent, they were for my situation and my baby, my poor baby who had a mother who may not be able to take proper care of him alone and a father who wanted to deny his existence.

My mum looked across at me suspiciously, but I ignored her glances. I ignored them all, wondering how these were my family, my circle, when we had nothing in common and no desire to scratch beneath the surface to find something.

I was an only child. My mother had me young and my father had married her. They were kind people and always took care of me. I wasn't abused or neglected, and my childhood wasn't bad, and yet it wasn't good either. It just kind of *was*.

As I grew up, they seemed relieved to be regaining their independence. I was sure they'd never planned on having children, but they'd ended up with me and made the best of it. When I looked at our wider family, they all parented the same, but me, I had wanted more. I'd had a few boyfriends and none of them were my forever guy, they had left me in no doubt that I wouldn't love like my parents had. Any children I had would be loved unconditionally, explicitly and they would never feel apathy from me in my role as their parent.

By the time I refocused on my surroundings, I had composed myself a little and was able to offer my parents, aunts, uncles and cousins a small smile. It was reciprocated as we dispersed from the graveyard and moved to the pub, the same one where I was staying.

Everyone sat in the bar and I found myself sitting with my parents who asked how I was and how things were?

I wasn't really sure how to answer either question, one, because I didn't really want to discuss those things with them and two, because I had no clue how I was or how things were.

Instead, I offered them a standard kind of, good thanks, fine. I couldn't say if they believed that or not, but they accepted it without question and went on to discuss a holiday they were planning to take in a few weeks.

My assembled family sat there with a sandwich, pork pie, fairy cake and a drink. Some of them shared stories of my grandmother and others simply listened, which seemed pretty standard funeral etiquette.

One by one they all left and headed home and when my parents left, I can't say that I felt anything aside from apathy. I did hope it wasn't hereditary or contagious, the apathy. I liked people who cared, who wore their heart on their sleeves. Honest people who were passionate and made no excuses for it. People like Seb. The person I was when I was with him. I sighed. I wouldn't be that person again because I was no longer with Seb.

I sat alone in the bar for another ten minutes or so when I became aware of someone standing nearby, watching me. Looking up, I found a pair of familiar dark eyes holding my gaze, Daryl.

Daryl had been my first serious boyfriend and I had loved him in that first love kind of way. He had been the first person who had openly shown me affection and I had been drawn to that like a moth to a flame. He was tall, dark and broad, a little brooding but that only added to the attraction initially, but by the end that had been a real turn-off. His brooding had become controlling and moody. He was one of the reasons I had left here and maybe one of the reasons I didn't come back very often.

He was heading for the table I sat at and once there, without waiting for an invitation, he sat down opposite me.

"I heard about your grandma."

I nodded. I had nothing to say to that, nothing to say to him. Of course he'd heard about her, this was a small village and everyone knew one another and in turn tended to know their business. That was something else I didn't miss about village life.

"Are you okay? You look okay."

I laughed at that, unlike Daryl who frowned at my amusement. Most people offered apologies when someone died, but not Daryl.

"I'm fine, thanks. You?"

"I guess. Why did you go?"

And there it was. I had left here five years ago and never looked back.

"I was worried about you when I found you were missing. Your parents had no clue where you were and didn't seem bothered about that."

I felt guilty. For the first time in forever I thought about what I'd done. Things between me and Daryl were bad by the time I left. Everything I did was under his gaze and scrutiny. He never hit me or called me vile names, but he was demanding and always needed to know where I was and what I was doing. More than that, he insisted on knowing who I was with.

I'd been sixteen when we got together and was studying to be a nursery nurse at college. He was a couple of years older and was a mechanic in the local garage. By the time I was halfway through my final year at college he was talking about me moving into his flat above the garage. I didn't want to. I was beginning to see that our relationship was flawed and that Daryl would only become more controlling and isolate me if we lived together. One night I went out with some friends from college to a club in a nearby town. There was a large group of us and some people brought boyfriends and girlfriends with them. I didn't. Daryl found out where we were, and gate crashed. When he arrived, I was dancing with one of my friend's boyfriends, innocently, but that's not how Daryl saw it. He kicked off big style and pummelled this guy into the middle of the following week and then dragged me home.

His intensity and desire to watch over me became worse after that and because of his behaviour I lost a few friends and those I hung onto didn't invite me out anymore.

Daryl made plans for me to move in after I finished college, but on my last day of college I went home, packed a small case and with the money I'd saved from working in the village store at the weekend, I waited for nightfall and then I ran, never to return on a permanent basis.

"Sorry."

My apology was unconvincing and why wouldn't it be? It was insincere. I wasn't sorry for leaving, not that I thought through how it may make Daryl feel. I did what I did for me and me alone.

"Are you back now? We could go on a date."

I smiled at the man opposite me as he blushed, something I didn't think I'd ever witnessed before.

"I still live in the flat over the garage. You could come round. Not much has changed there. Not much has changed anywhere. I still think about you, you know, you and me. I know we were young, but we're older now. I could take care of you."

I stared at him, no longer smiling. *I could take care of you. Not much has changed.* He'd said the latter twice, in relation to his flat and anywhere. He was wrong though because I had changed, and I was not prepared to go back in time or in character. And as for him taking care of me, well, that kind of care I didn't need. My life might have been a bit of a mess right now, but it wasn't that much of a mess and it was a mess I could and would sort out. I didn't know how, but I would.

"Don't say no." He got to his feet. "Eight o'clock tonight, I'll pick you up. I won't take no for an answer."

He turned and left with his words ringing in my head, *I won't take no for an answer*, or maybe it was alarm bells ringing in my head.

****

I headed up to my room and tried to absorb my encounter with Daryl. I didn't want to go to his flat or see him or talk to him. I could stay here, lock myself in and refuse to answer the door, but that was unlikely to work. He'd probably just barge in anyway. I was tired, although there was no way I would sleep, not even a nap, knowing Daryl was on the prowl.

There was only one thing to do, go home. There really was nothing for me here, nothing I wanted here, and whilst there may not be a Seb waiting for me at home, I needed to get my shit together and see him. He needed to know that I was keeping the baby and that I would never stand in his way to have a relationship with him or her, but what I wouldn't allow would be for him to be the sort of parent who flitted in and out of their child's life. Someone who would be apathetic. No, that was a hard limit for me, and he needed to know and understand that.

I switched on my phone and called for a taxi, ignoring the dozens of messages from Carrie, and the voicemails and missed calls from Seb. I did, however return the one from Sophie who was asking me if there was any chance I could return to work tomorrow. I sent her a quick text, confirming that I could and would work, then headed downstairs with my bag I hadn't really unpacked. Like a fugitive, I scurried to the back of the pub where I'd asked the taxi to wait and then, for the second time in my life, I ran away under the cover of night, but this time I knew exactly where I was going and why.

****

The following morning when I woke, I quickly got ready for work and headed out. I text Carrie a simple message to confirm that I was okay and back at work but would call her later to chat.

I rolled my phone in my hand and considered calling Seb, but I didn't really have time to chat as I had just arrived at work, so I decided to wait until I got home.

The sight that greeted me when I entered the house where I worked was a little chaotic. The kitchen was a mess, with breakfast things strewn everywhere. Maurice looked like a lost soul while the children literally ran circles around him.

"Where's Sophie?" I asked, expecting her to be there as she'd asked me to work.

Maurice shook his head. "Gone. Not coming back. I'm glad you're here. Thank you." He stepped forward and reached for me, folding me in his arms and very briefly he hugged me.

Maybe I shouldn't have said I'd work, but then I hadn't known what I was coming back to, had I?

Chapter Thirty-Three

Seb

I arrived first for lunch, but Gabe was only a few minutes behind me. He approached me and took a seat opposite.

"Lunch is on you," he said seriously, his brow furrowing into a frown.

I stared across at him, silently imploring him to explain.

"I have been in the shit since you left my house the other afternoon."

"Ah."

"Ah, yeah, that doesn't even scratch the surface. She silently fumed for hours, until Charlotte went to bed and then she let rip."

"Was it because you hadn't told her about just how closely related we all are and that Imogen was mine?"

"No, she was cool about that." He laughed. "She respected our past and the intrinsic details of our friendships and relationships. What she objected to was me dismissing her, what she saw as my defence of your actions, which are still unacceptable."

I shrugged, unable to deny that.

"And what she viewed as me taking your side over hers."

"I guess she was hurt by that." I had no clue how Nanny had felt but thought I ought to offer something.

"A little, but more than that she was pissed off. She left me in no doubt that I was in the doghouse and that if I ever, and I quote, excluded her, dismissed her or treated her like the hired help, I would have to start considering the sofa as my new bed."

I laughed. I did like Nanny and her take no shit attitude. She was scarier as a wife than she'd ever been as a nanny and employee of Gabe's.

"Well I'm fucking glad you're amused by my newlywed status going to shit."

"Aww, didn't you get any Nanny special love?"

He flipped me off making me laugh louder and harder.

"That's a no then."

"A firmer no than you could even imagine. I am waiting on her hand and foot and if all of my deliveries have arrived, we may be able to open our own florists."

I said nothing but did smirk again.

"Now, to wipe your face clear of any amusement. What's happening with you and Bea?"

My face dropped. "She hasn't replied to my calls or voicemails, not a word."

Gabe looked concerned. His expression matched how I felt perfectly.

"I don't want to bombard her or for her to feel I'm harassing her."

"That makes sense," he agreed. "You could text her. I don't know if that will make a difference, but it can't hurt, can it?"

I had wanted to speak to her, not do this over text, but if she was intent on ignoring my calls, I might not have much of a choice.

I pulled my phone out and composed the message carefully.

<Hi, am really not hassling you and I get you're mad at me. I am mad at me. Could we meet and talk. We really need to talk. I promise not to be a dickhead. Sorry, I hope the funeral went okay and that you are okay. Just say when and where and I will be there. X>

I offered Gabe a look at my screen and once he'd read it, he nodded. I wasn't sure how much more I could or should say before we were face to face. I hit send and Gabe and I ordered lunch. Conversation was slightly strained, mainly because we were both avoiding subjects like Nanny, babies and anything emotional.

Lunch was delivered when my phone vibrated on the table. Gabe stared across as I looked at it. I read the message, re-read it and then read it aloud to my friend.

<Hi. We do need to talk and face to face is best. I was going to call you when I finished work. I'm quite busy so will call you later, when I get home. X>

My friend and I stared at each other.

"At least she sent you a kiss," he said.

"Don't girls send a kiss to everyone?" I was sure most did and knew Bea did.

Gabe shrugged. "I dunno, but they don't send kisses to men they have given up on."

He was right and although it was a small thing, it gave me hope, hope that Bea and I might be able to move forward somehow.

I went back to my office where I had a quiet afternoon. It gave me the time to think about things…my past and hopefully my future. I re-read Bea's message and wondered why she was at work. I was certain she hadn't been due home until today, so why was she at work? Thinking of her being at work, I remembered what Nanny had said about her boss trying it on. How fucking dare he! He was her boss and she looked after his kids. I pushed thoughts from my mind that told me I was hypocritical as my friend had started a relationship with his nanny, but Carrie hadn't had a boyfriend. Bea had. Me.

A thought began to form in my mind. Bea planned on calling me and was in agreement that we should meet, face to face, and we would, tonight. I was going to wind up work for the day, then after I'd gone home and showered and changed, I would meet Bea, pick her up from work, we could chat. And if the chance to introduce myself to her boss who thought it was okay to try it on with her presented itself, then I'd take it. I could put a face to Maurice's name and leave him in no doubt that his days of making passes at my girlfriend were behind him.

Chapter Thirty-Four

Bea

After agreeing to call Seb after work and also acknowledging that we should meet and talk face to face, I felt a mixture of nerves and relief. What if he was going to walk away from me and the baby for good, or give me the ultimatum of him or the baby? I mean, there was no choice to make as far as I was concerned, the baby would always be my choice, no matter how much I loved Seb or how much better he made me.

The children were drawing and colouring at the table outdoors. In fact, I was drawing and colouring with them. I wasn't much of an artist so tended to stick to shapes or simple flowers.

We were all engrossed in our tasks so that when a shadow fell across us, we all jumped. The shadow was Maurice. He smiled down at us all and even sat with us once he'd cast his jacket aside. He smiled at me and it seemed natural and somehow familiar rather than as if he was trying to impress me or show some attraction.

It was about half an hour later with our artwork complete that Maurice took the children indoors to find somewhere to display their pictures. I went to follow, but he waved for me to stay where I was.

"Why don't I make us all a drink and we could have a chat, Bea." His words were almost phrased as a question, but they carried an air of authority that suggested I should stay where I was and wait for my drink.

The children returned with their father and a tray of soft drinks, but unlike their father who sat back down, the children ran around the garden.

"How are you, Bea?"

I stared at the man opposite me wondering what that question meant.

"Fine, thank you."

He smiled. "Sorry, I've startled you with my friendly chatting."

I laughed, thinking that he had, but I might need to get used to it if Sophie didn't return. "A little, and I'm sorry too for making it so obvious."

"Shall we start again?"

I nodded, and we did start again. He asked how the children had been and if there was anything I needed to help with my job. We talked about TV, music, books and generally chatted. Finally, he explained that he would now be the children's primary carer. Sophie would have open access, but for now that may be minimal as she was intent on discovering herself. He arched a brow at the last two words, and I laughed at his expression.

"Could she not discover herself with the children?" As soon as my question was out, I could have kicked myself. Not only was it unprofessional but it was also a little judgemental and Sophie had always been kind to me.

Maurice didn't seem to have an issue with my question. He smiled and shrugged. "You'd think so, hope so, wouldn't you? But it seems not. I just hope that once she has discovered herself, she doesn't find that person isn't a mother because my children don't deserve that. If she decides she's not a wife, which I think is a forgone conclusion, that is all about me and her, but the children…" He trailed off sadly.

"Yeah. Children really are innocent in these things, aren't they, or they should be." I was back to thinking about me and Seb and our baby again.

He nodded. "Let me try this one again, then. How are you, Bea?"

This time I wasn't taken aback by his question, but I was

taken aback by the tears that suddenly filled my eyes.

Maurice reached across and took my hand in his. "Is there anything I can do to help?"

I shook my head, there was nothing he could do, nothing anyone could do except Seb. "I'm pregnant." I hadn't planned on telling him and certainly not the way I just had.

"I see." He rubbed the back of my hand. "And the father?"

I shrugged, causing my boss to look really quite alarmed.

"No, gosh, no. I know who he is." I laughed. "But he doesn't appear to want a baby."

"Oh dear. What a pair we are. You're having a baby with a man who doesn't want to be a father, and I have children with a woman who is deciding if she wants to be a mother."

I cringed at his summing up but didn't disagree.

"What will you do?" He asked and although me leaving to have a baby could be problematic for him, I didn't get the impression that his thoughts and concerns were for anyone other than me.

"I'm not sure, not beyond the fact that I am having the baby, with or without the father. We need to talk about it some more."

Maurice nodded. "Maybe once the shock wears off. I assume it wasn't planned."

I shook my head again. "Not at all so it really was a shock, for us both."

"Then maybe he needs some time, unless he's a bit of a no hoper."

"I only have a certain amount of time left to give him, but he isn't a no hoper." I smiled as I thought of Seb, my feelings for him and our baby. I wondered if it would be a boy or a girl, would it look like one of us or a mixture of us both?

"Will you be able to manage financially?" Maurice's very sensible question brought me down to earth with a bump.

"I'm not sure how, but I'll have to, won't I?"

"Bloody hell!" he suddenly blurted out. "I'm going to have to find a new nanny while you're on leave."

I laughed at his horrified expression. "Sorry."

"Don't be. It's a wonderful thing to have a child. Maybe you could help me find someone to cover for you and show them the ropes."

"Okay." I smiled a little sadly at the idea of someone taking over my role here.

"Bea, your job is safe here, don't ever worry about that. In fact, I might have a proposition for you that would fulfil both of our needs."

Chapter Thirty-Five

Seb

When I arrived at the house where Bea worked, I parked up and sat and waited. I was early. Very early, but that was better than risking missing her. I hoped she'd be pleased to see me and not pissed off that I had rocked up here unannounced.

With an hour to kill I listened to music, then switched to the radio before checking my phone over and over again. I flicked through the little social media I had and then resorted to downloading a game where I bounced a ball at matching coloured balls. I could see how people became a little obsessed with these things, but my only obsession was in the house I was in front of so the bouncy ball thing only distracted me for a short time.

My phone alert told me I had a message, Nanny.

<I hope you and Bea can work something out. Even when you're a dick, I love you. I want you to be happy, you and Bea and if it can't be together, please make it right for you both, for all of you. X>

Fucking hell! Gabe had clearly told his wife of my plans. Maybe telling her that worked better than the dozens and dozens of flowers he'd ordered in a bid to apologise. I laughed at his plight in the doghouse. I loved Nanny, loved how happy she made my friend, even when she was giving him shit, and the way she loved my niece was an honour to watch, but she was a ballbreaker. She was basically telling me I was a dick but needed to be less of a dick if I was ditching her friend who was pregnant with my baby. I wasn't ditching anyone, but she was right about one thing, this was no longer about just me and Bea. There was an innocent baby stuck in the middle. My baby. That scared me more than anything and yet I knew I would never walk away from my child, but would I be able to love him or her as I had Imogen?

<Thanks, Nanny. I love you too. Don't tell you husband I love you or he'll get all pissy about it. You know how jealous he gets. In fact, tell him, tell him now lol. Also tell him how great the name Seb is for a boy...your boy, his boy X>

With my phone in my pocket and itchy feet, I got out of my car and headed to the house. It was only a couple of minutes before Bea should finish work, so I would be there to ensure she didn't stay over.

I climbed the steps to the door and was about to knock when I heard laughter and voices coming from around the back of the house. I followed the path at the side of the property that led me to the garden and the source of the sounds, the children playing and Bea sitting at a table with a man, presumably her boss. He was probably only a few years older than me, and slightly rounder, but he was tall, dark and I supposed attractive in a dark skinned, Mediterranean way.

Staring through the wrought iron gate I had a ringside seat to everything and was close enough to hear them too. He held her hand across the table and that had rage whooshing through my veins until my ears felt as though they may burst. She did nothing to pull away, but it looked like a gesture of comfort more than anything else, but still, I was pissed off beyond belief and then I heard him speak.

"Bea, your job is safe here, don't ever worry about that. In fact, I might have a proposition for you that would fulfil both of our needs."

I could barely believe my ears and had a very good idea what his proposition would look like. With a deep breath and a good dose of self-control, I did not march in and lay him out in his own garden. I continued my deep breathing and waited to hear what he was offering, and then I would lay him out in his own garden.

"Maurice—" Bea began but he cut her off.

"Let me finish, please."

She said nothing but nodded her head.

"With Sophie gone, I'm going to need more help, especially evenings and weekends."

I saw Bea tense and pull her hand away. Thank fuck!

Maurice continued, "We have separate accommodation over the garage that was originally intended for family or friends coming to stay, but none of them come all that often. It is completely self-contained and is yours for the taking, but in exchange, I'd need more."

I was ready to burst in and spread his fucking nose across his face. He was speaking to his employee, but more than that, he was speaking to my girlfriend. My pregnant girlfriend, although he was unlikely to know that.

"And with the baby on the way, it would remove the issue of a suitable home and rent."

Okay, clearly he knew about the baby. That pissed me off too.

"You wouldn't have to commute, meaning you could be more flexible in your hours."

Bea raised her hand, to stop him speaking. Thank fuck.

"Maurice, I can't be a surrogate parent to your children and would still need time off and time where I wasn't on call."

He nodded. Smug prick. I was raging.

"Of course. That's not what I am suggesting. You move in, live-in. I will get a second nanny who you could help to settle and show her the ropes. You could work the hours between you and then, when you go on leave, she will take over. It might even be that once you return to work you might want to reduce your working hours and I could facilitate that for you."

I hated the way he said *for you,* but it was a good offer he was making, so long as there were no strings. I wasn't convinced there weren't.

"That's a lot to consider, plus, what would I do with the baby once I returned to work? It would defeat the object to come back to work caring for your children if someone else was caring for my own."

No way in hell was that happening.

"You could bring the baby with you. That wouldn't be an issue at all."

"Wow."

She was tempted, and why wouldn't she be? As a single parent this would be a perfect solution, but it would also be a perfect way for Maurice to worm his way into Bea's affections, not to mention her pants. So, thank you arsehole, but no thank you because she won't be a single parent.

"Think about it."

He was persistent, I'd give him that, and sounded all too reasonable.

"Thank you. I will."

Like fuck she would.

Bea suddenly checked the time and got to her feet. "I should be getting off and thank you again."

Maurice stood and moved to stand next to her. Was he going to kiss her? No, but the fucker pulled her in for a hug. This was my moment. I needed to introduce fucking Maurice and his too good to be true offer to Bea's boyfriend and I was going to do that right now.

Chapter Thirty-Six

Bea

Maurice's offer really might have been the answer to my prayers, but I needed to think about it properly and maybe discuss it with Carrie who would be able to offer some insight into the pros and cons of living-in as a nanny. Although, hers and Gabe's relationship was very different to mine and Maurice's and always had been. Plus, I needed to speak to Seb before I made any big decisions that involved our baby. If he chose to turn his back on us again then Maurice's offer might be the best choice all round. If he didn't, if he wanted to be a daddy, even without being a boyfriend then I would need to listen to his opinions and thoughts before making a decision.

I glanced down at my watch and realised it was past the end of my workday. I got to my feet and Maurice did the same before moving to stand next to me and then he pulled me in for an unexpected hug. While his hug didn't feel uncomfortable, I needed to get off and make plans to meet Seb.

"Stranger danger, stranger danger," shouted Craig as the sound of the gate rattling sounded.

Maurice and I both turned in the direction of the gate. Maybe I didn't need to make plans to meet Seb after all. My eyes landed on a cross looking Seb standing in the now open gateway. He wasn't the only cross one here. What the fuck was he doing here, anyway? As he entered, my question was answered.

"Hi." He offered an outstretched hand to Maurice, a hand he

accepted, not even knowing who the stranger before him was. "Sebastian Oakes, Dr Sebastian Oakes, actually, Bea's boyfriend."

I glared at him. How fucking dare he! Just who did he think he was, coming here like this? His reason was to clearly introduce himself to Maurice and in doing so flex his male ego muscles. His sole intention was to show my boss who was really in charge here, or so he thought. And what the fuck was with the use of his professional title? I had never heard him refer to himself that way. I'd also never heard him call himself Sebastian either. Arsehole.

"Ah." Maurice got it too, meaning I now had embarrassment to add to my earlier anger. "Nice to meet you." He turned to Craig and Rosie, "We're safe kids, no stranger, this is Bea's boyfriend."

Seb had the audacity to move next to me and drape an arm around my middle before landing a kiss to my temple. I reacted to his kiss and touch on a visceral level, but my emotional state turned into silently fuming rage at his appearance and behaviour. Thank fuck Maurice didn't counter-react in the same way or Seb's next move might have been to piss all over me to stake his claim and show his dominance.

I'd really had enough. "I'll see you all in the morning." I gave the kids a hug then turned to Maurice. "Thank you, for everything, and I really will consider your very kind and generous offer." I reached towards him, and mainly to piss Seb off, I put my hand on his arm and rubbed it before giving it a small squeeze then grabbed my bag from the kitchen and exited via the back gate Seb had earlier breached.

I saw his car as soon as I got to the roadside and rather than stand by it and wait for Seb, I walked on by. I was so angry with his show of machismo and dickheadedness rolled into one that I couldn't be trusted to speak to him, nor to be in an enclosed space such as a car. My phone buzzed and although I expected it to be Seb, it wasn't, it was Carrie.

<Hi, let me know when you're free for a catch up. I've missed you and am worried about you. X>

I replied a short and to the point response.

<Yeah, me too. I'm fine and I'll call you later or in the morning to sort something out. X>

With my phone slipped into my pocket, I carried on stomping down the road.

"Get in the car." Seb had pulled up alongside me at the kerbside.

"Not on your life." I carried on walking without pause or hesitation.

"Bea, get in the car."

He sounded pissed off. That made two of us.

"Kiss my arse." And still I carried on walking.

Seb continued to drive slowly next to me. "You are testing my fucking patience."

I stopped dead and glared in the open car window at him. "Your patience? What about mine? You are unbelievable, Dr Sebastian Oakes."

"Get in the car, now."

I shook my head and turned slightly as if to take a short cut through a gully that ran between the allotments and the back end of the park where Carrie and I often took the children.

"Don't you dare go down there. Anybody could be lying in wait."

If I hadn't been so angry, I would have laughed at that, but I was, so I didn't. Instead, I flipped him off and headed down the gully.

By the time I came out the other end he was there, still driving along.

"You are going to be reported for kerb crawling if you continue doing this," I warned him without even looking at him.

He put the car into gear and zoomed off, stopping a short distance down the road to park. I was confused as to what he was doing until I saw him get out and watched as he stalked back up the road with only me in sight.

Coming to a stop in front of me, and without a word being

uttered, he reached for me and threw me over his shoulder to carry me back to his car where I expected him to unceremoniously throw me into the passenger seat. He didn't. As he lowered me in his touch took on a gentleness I hadn't expected and he placed me into the seat with care.

"Stay. We need to talk. Now."

Chapter Thirty-Seven

Seb

Relief washed over me when Bea made no attempt to get out of the car. I was entirely aware that she could have gotten out at any point and I would have been incapable of stopping her as I was behind the wheel.

All of that led me to the conclusion that she wanted to be there, with me and knew we needed to talk and sort this out. However, just in case I was wrong, and she was ready to bolt, I drove us to my home.

As soon as I pulled up outside, Bea got out of the car and slammed the door before standing at the front door where she glared at me. My earlier amusement at my friend being in the doghouse faded as I realised I was in one too, but feared it was going to take a lot more than a house full of flowers to get out of it.

Once I opened the door, I attempted to place a hand on Bea's hip to usher her in. She immediately pulled away, seemingly not wanting my touch. I allowed her to put some distance between us by marching through the house ahead of me. I knew I was going to need to pitch this conversation right before it got blown out of the water completely so needed to be patient.

"Would you like some tea?" I asked as soon as we were through the front door. Even I couldn't make tea inflammatory, could I?

"What do you want?" She ignored my question and sounded mighty pissed, so maybe I could make tea inflammatory.

"We need to talk—"

She cut me off completely. "Then talk, go ahead. I mean, it's not like I have a choice or an opinion in any of this, is it?"

"Of course you do—"

Again, she cut me off. "No, because if I did you wouldn't have barged into my work and acted like a dickhead, although if you had an ounce of respect for me you wouldn't have fucking walked out on me without a look back when I told you I was pregnant."

"I am making tea and then we can talk. I will talk to start with and maybe you will understand."

She glared at me as I left her to head into the kitchen where I made tea. When I returned, she was at least sitting down and looked a little more relaxed...not much, but a little.

I passed her a cup and offered her a chocolate biscuit, her favourites. She arched a brow, knowing that I was on a major suck up mission.

"I'm sorry." That was my opening gambit.

She looked across at me sitting in the seat opposite her. She waited. I was unsure for what, so said nothing, just in case I made this worse.

"For what? What are you sorry for, Seb? For getting me pregnant? Checking if it was yours? For telling me I couldn't be and that we couldn't have a baby? Maybe for walking out on me with the assurance that you weren't doing this? Or perhaps that you didn't text or call or check in again before I went to my grandmother's funeral? It could even be for the fact that you came to my place of work, uninvited and made me feel ridiculous by making yourself look more ridiculous. If it's none of them I am left with it being your even more ridiculous pursuit of me that ended in you physically manhandling me, pregnant until I was in your car? So, please, clarify, what exactly are you sorry for?"

I had clearly fucked up badly judging by my list of crimes that she was well versed in and not backwards in pointing them out, naming each and every one of them.

"Princess—"

Yet again she cut me off and I was tiring of that.

154

"Don't you dare call me that. You only get to call me that if your actions back it up and over the last few days you haven't treated me like a princess, so, you don't get to call me one."

"Fucking fine. I am sorry, for everything. Every single thing you listed and a hundred more things beside. I have fucked up, I get it, loud and clear, but if we have any chance of me explaining my actions, as deplorable as you may consider them, then you need to listen and I need to talk."

She nodded, petulantly.

"And that means you'll need to let me speak without fucking interrupting."

She glared but offered another nod, a reluctant one this time.

"The news of your pregnancy knocked me for six. I had no clue how to process the information or the reality of it. I handled my reaction badly and my behaviour was awful, I know that, but there was a reason for it, I swear." I heard my voice wobble with emotion; sadness, regret, fear, grief, loss and many others I couldn't name, and then I took a very deep breath and braced myself for what would either be the best or worst outcome.

I talked for what felt like hours. Thousands of words spilled from my mouth, starting with one word, a name, Imogen. I told Bea all about my marriage, my sister, my baby, her death and my subsequent divorce. My voice remained flat for all of it as I recited facts and details, as if I was a journalist reporting a piece of news.

That's the strange thing with grief, everyone's experience was different and there was no wrong or right way of dealing with it, not really. I accepted it and moved on, shutting my baby girl away in a special place in my heart and mind, with a vow to never let her out again or indeed, let anyone in. She was mine to love and mourn. Maybe that made me a selfish bastard, but I didn't care, that was the only way I could cope.

It was no wonder that after Imogen's death my marriage to Cheryl crumbled. She was different to me and she wanted, needed to talk and I was happy for her to do that. I even found professionals she could talk to as well as family and friends, but that wasn't enough, she wanted to talk to me. She wanted, maybe needed us to share our grief, our loss of the child that was ours together. Her attempts to force me to do so were countless. Day after day, week after week, she would open a conversation with Imogen, memories, hopes and dreams we'd had for her, but I was incapable of giving anything back. Cheryl filled our home with photos and mementos of the short time we'd been parents and with each addition and every conversation broached, I died a little more inside. Our marriage broke down further until there was nothing left to work with. The love I'd had for my wife died, maybe at the second my daughter had and the more she tried to reignite it by joining our grief the more I withdrew. I couldn't do that to myself, so it fell apart. Everything fell apart.

I explained all of this to Bea and then, when I thought she understood what I had endured, I moved on to her telling me she was pregnant and why I reacted in the way I had.

"I was scared. Fucking petrified to open myself up to that possibility, never mind the reality. I couldn't risk loving someone that much, that intensely or that unconditionally again in case I lost them, like I had with Imogen. I barely survived it the first time so I know a second time would kill me. If not physically, I would die inside."

I risked looking up to face Bea. I felt wetness on my face as my own tears flowed, only to find the woman opposite me crying too.

"I'm sorry," she said and that saw me completely falling apart because she had absolutely nothing to be sorry for, not a single thing.

Chapter Thirty-Eight

Bea

Stunned. That is how I felt, and yet that word seemed inadequate. Never in a million years would I have imagined the heart-breaking horror of what Seb had described as being his past. I knew very little of Gabe's first wife beyond her being dead and that was only recently acquired knowledge. Nobody spoke of her and they certainly didn't discuss the details of her now obvious mental health issues and the circumstances of her death. Charlotte occasionally mentioned that she'd had a mummy whose belly she grew in, but that was pretty much it. I imagined that might increase once the little girl discovered Carrie's pregnancy.

I stared across at Seb and had no clue what to say or do. Tears streaked my own face and the image of him was somewhat blurred, courtesy of the fresh ones welling in my eyes. He was distressed and I wanted to help him in any way I could. His behaviour towards me and news of my shocking pregnancy had still been wrong, but at least I had some understanding now of why it had triggered such an extreme reaction. That could all wait though. For now, he needed something more. Compassion and comfort.

What could I say to make this less painful? Probably nothing, but I'd try. "I'm sorry."

He shook his head as the last word left my mouth and then he disintegrated before my eyes. His tears took on a life of their own, far too many to control and along with them came a series of sobs and choking noises that had him shaking uncontrollably.

Without any thought, I got to my feet and moved to stand in front of the space where he sat. "Babe."

He looked up at me and my heart broke a little for him. Slowly, with care, I climbed into his lap and with my arms wrapped around him I pulled him close and held him, rocked him, offered him as much comfort as I possessed.

Seconds turned into minutes that he cried for. No words were exchanged and then, eventually silence fell over us.

"Sorry," Seb began.

"No. You have nothing to be sorry for." I assumed he was apologising for his emotional outburst.

"I do. For how I treated you when you told me you were pregnant. I'm sorry," he repeated.

I nodded my acceptance of his apology. "And I really am sorry that you lost your baby and had to endure that pain. I can't even imagine that..." I heard the break in my voice but was desperate not to cry because it was his pain and loss, not mine.

"It's not something I talk about and is why I vowed no serious relationships or marriage or babies."

"Where does that leave us?" I didn't want to make his past about my present, but I really needed to know.

"Well, it leaves you in my lap, pregnant with our baby after I gate-crashed you at work to let your boss know he needs to find someone else to make passes at because you are my girlfriend and completely out of bounds for him."

I frowned down at him from my slightly elevated position. I hadn't told him about my boss making a pass at me, in fact the only person I'd told was Carrie. "We really need to discuss boundaries..." I seemed to suddenly hear the words he'd spoken. "Is that what I am, your girlfriend?"

He nodded, still sniffing due to his earlier upset.

"If you want to be. If you'll have me, both of you?" He placed his hand on my still flat belly.

"I've always wanted you." I was the one sniffing now, sniffing back happy tears.

"Pinky promise."

With a sudden grin, I extended my finger to his and we

shook.

"Do you suppose Maurice got the message that you're having my baby and you're the girl I love?"

I was sure all of the air had been sucked from the room, or at least my lungs. He loved me. I was the girl he loved, that's what he'd said. "Do you? Do you love me?"

Long seconds passed as I waited for him to reply. I physically tensed, as if I was somehow trying to brace myself for the impact of him withdrawing his declaration of love.

"I do. A lot. More than is probably healthy. I wasn't sure how much until these last few days. But, yes, I love you, which is a good job as we're having a baby…assuming you want a baby with me now that you've seen what a dick I can be."

I nodded, my tears flowing freely, happy tears. "I love you, too, and without you I was having this baby, so with you is a definite yes. And yes, you can be a real dick, but you're my dick."

He laughed. "I certainly am."

A dark tension fell and before I'd thought of anything else, I was pressing down, my crotch against his and my lips were dropping to his, gently kissing him, and then it turned more serious and deeper. The meshing and moulding of lips became more frantic with tongues doing battle for supremacy as clothes seemed to fall away until we were both panting and topless.

We ended up lying together on the sofa, kissing, touching, stroking and caressing. One of Seb's hands found my newly sensitive breasts and with a finger and thumb rolling and pinching the nipple of it, I writhed beneath him. His head dropped so that he could draw my hard and throbbing tip into the wondrous wet heat of his mouth, while his hand transferred its attention and grip to the other. I was in agony and ecstasy at the same time and it felt amazing.

Our clothing on our bottom halves was being cast aside, leaving me in just pants and Seb completely naked, his hard and leaking arousal desperate to find my core and its release. We rolled around each other a little, changing and swapping positions until we finally settled lying on our sides, Seb behind me, holding me tight, and then his hand that had been on my hip moved over and down until it infiltrated the tiny barrier of my pants.

Chapter Thirty-Nine

Seb

The feel of Bea's soft and dampening folds beneath my hand was like hitting the fucking jackpot. Her heat was going to burn me in every way possible because nothing felt better or more natural than this, being with her, touching her.

Her moans grew louder as I drove her on towards her release.

"Babe," she groaned as she reached behind her, desperate to get her hands on me, to hold on when the world came crashing around her.

"Come on, Princess," I encouraged as her muscles clenched around my fingers that were buried inside her.

"Yes, yes," she cried and then in a series of calls and moans she came, squeezing my digits while the nails of one hand dug in and clawed my leg.

I coaxed her down then cast her pants aside and deliberated how to do this. My dick was beyond hard and was already leaking pre-cum. Looking down at the beautiful image of Bea lying in front of me, I smiled. A smile of relief that I hadn't lost her. A smile because she was beautiful, basking in the afterglow of post-orgasmic release, her mouth slightly open and her eyes closed, looking perfect. And a smile of hope for the future, for us both and the life that was currently growing inside her.

She shifted her position so that her leg was draped back across my hip, opening her up and inviting me in. I didn't need asking twice, that was for sure. Slowly, I spread her a little more and slid inside her, then held still. We lay there, together, coupled and neither of us spoke, we simply enjoyed the moment. After probably only a few seconds I began to move, slowly at first, leisurely almost, but as with all things me and Bea, the calm didn't last. Before long we were both panting heavily, moving in perfect rhythm, my orgasm getting closer and closer as I became aware of a change in Bea's breathing that coincided with her internal muscles squeezing around me once more, preparing to come with me.

Instinctively my hand dropped from her hip and came to rest on her tummy, where our tiny baby was safely encased, growing and developing and I suddenly realised that this was everything I wanted and I really did want it all with the woman who was now falling apart around me, and with that I joined her.

****

I sat in just a pair of jeans, Bea wore my t-shirt eating cereal while we watched something crappy on TV. Bea was texting Carrie between eating and taking in some details of the docu-drama thing that was on the screen. She looked calm, happy and comfortable as she chatted with her friend from my sofa.

My own phone sounded, and it was no surprise to see Gabe's name light up my screen.

<How do you do it, you jammy sod? You fucked up big style and yet you are back in your girlfriend's good books and I get the impression from my wife's giggling and smirking that you got lucky too. Me? Even with the flowers that are in every room in my house (I might have gone over the top) I am still in the doghouse and currently very unlucky...unlikely to be getting lucky before this baby is born at this rate.>

I laughed loudly at my friend's message and plight.

<Wow, Nanny holds a grudge and plays hard ball, much like yours will be, hard and blue >

I laughed even louder when his response of a single emoji of the middle finger flipping me off landed.

Bea needed to go home as she had no clothes at mine and had work the following day. As I drove her home I cautiously broached the subject of her work, Maurice and his offer to her. I issued myself an internal warning that I needed to remain calm or we'd end up arguing again.

"So, Maurice's offer?" It took all of my powers of control not to sneer his name or sound angry.

"What about it?"

I couldn't believe that was her actual response to my very reasonable comment. My irritation was already rising so I hoped her next words were going to be more reasonable.

"Exactly. What about it?"

"In case you hadn't noticed, I've been kind of busy since he made the offer."

That did at least make me smile as I recalled just how she'd been busy, with me. "Well, as I see it, the offer is null and void."

"Is it now?" She sounded disbelieving, but I was deadly serious.

"Princess," I said through near gritted teeth. "There is no way my pregnant girlfriend and then my girlfriend and baby are living with another man and his family."

She flicked a glance my way but said nothing as I pulled up outside her home.

"Tell me you are fucking with me because it won't be happening, Bea."

"Seb, I'll let you know when I've made a decision because the baby and I will need to live somewhere, and I need work but can't afford the cost of childcare."

I stared at her agog. How did she think this was going to work, me, her and our baby, our family? Well, I knew how it was going to work. We were going to share a home and she didn't need to worry about work or childcare, not that I objected to her working if that's what she wanted, but the cost of childcare was not an issue. Sadness washed over me as I considered anyone looking after my child, anyone who wasn't me or her. I knew it was irrational, but the one time Imogen was supposed to have been taken care of by someone who wasn't her parent she'd ended up dead.

"Hey." Bea's voice, full of concern, brought me back from that dark place. "Babe, you okay?"

"Yeah, sorry." I wasn't sure what I was sorry for exactly.

"No, I'm sorry. I was winding you up about Maurice and his offer. It was an amazing offer when I thought I was going to be raising this baby alone, but I'm not now, am I?"

"No, no, you're not, never. Pinky promise." I offered her my little finger and we shook on it.

Chapter Forty

Bea

A few weeks had passed since the day where Seb had appeared at my work and subsequently told me about his past. About his daughter who had so tragically died.

I had gone to work the next day and firstly apologised to Maurice for Seb's behaviour and assured him that my boyfriend wasn't usually that much of a dick, I'm paraphrasing. I also thanked him for his kind offer of a home but declined it. He was really cool about it actually. He did say that he still thought employing a new nanny before I went on maternity leave was a good idea and hoped I'd be happy to show her the ropes, which I was.

The idea of someone else taking over my role there didn't bother me as such, but I was concerned that I may not have a job to come back to. Maurice reassured me on that and Seb insisted that I wouldn't need to go back to work if I didn't want to. My relationship with my boss had returned to normal. Better than the way it had been. He was friendlier and more approachable, but not in a creepy way. He had apologised for making that pass at me and I truly believed and accepted his apology. He was a nice man and a good father who had been hurt, drunk and panicking at being the main parent in his children's life when previously he'd been the back-up parent.

All in all, life was good. Better than good. Seb and I spent pretty much every night together and although he was still coming to terms with being a father again and opening himself up to the pain that had brought him first time around, he was embracing it and beginning to look forward to it. Watching him with Charlotte, as I often did, showed me what a wonderful father he would be to our baby.

Carrie and Gabe were a great support to us both and we all got together regularly as well as me and Carrie meeting up several times in the week with the children. Carrie's pregnancy was a few weeks ahead of mine and she had the tiniest baby bump I was in true envy of. We were meeting at their home later and I was excited to tell her how my first ultrasound had gone.

"You okay there? Nervous?" Seb pulled my hand into his as we sat in the waiting room together.

"Maybe a little," I admitted.

Carrie and Gabe had scan photos all over their house now and knew their baby was growing and developing. They knew that everything was exactly as it should be and that is what I was desperate to know.

"Princess, this baby is going to be perfect."

I smiled at his reassurance and the glow he had seemed to develop when speaking about our baby.

"I mean, how could it be anything else with us as its parents?"

I laughed at his ability to show himself in this perfect light that I knew was a joke, but I had to agree that he was pretty perfect. With a squeeze of his hand, I rested my head on his shoulder. "Thank you."

He leaned down and kissed the top of my head. I wasn't sure if he knew that my gratitude was for him being there, for telling me about his past, for taking my mind off my own rising nerves or for the fact that in spite of him losing Imogen and his first-hand knowledge that not everything worked out perfectly, he was reassuring me that perfect existed for us. I thought that he did know, maybe not all of those reasons but some, most.

"Beatrice Piper?"

We both leapt to our feet when my name was called and followed the lady who stood in the doorway of the consultation room.

"Let's go and meet our baby."

We both grinned at Seb's words. This was about to get real.

****

There was no disguising our beaming smiles when we got to Carrie and Gabe's house. We had met our baby and he, or she, was perfect in every way. My pregnancy was on track and I had never been happier. Seb opened the door to his friend's house and walked in as if he belonged there. He called out to them as we entered the hallway where we found a very excited Charlotte bounding towards us.

Seb scooped her up in his arms and kissed her face all over, making her giggle. Carrie appeared behind her and then Gabe who immediately put an arm around his wife as they stopped and laughed at a giggling and flailing Charlotte.

"No, no, you're too prickly," laughed Charlotte while Seb continued his assault on her. "I'm going to wee," she squealed in protest.

Carrie laughed and warned Seb. "If I end up cleaning up a puddle of wee because of you and your prickly kisses, there will be trouble."

Seb put down Charlotte who immediately ran for the bathroom leaving the grown-ups together.

"Well?" Carrie was already at my side as I retrieved my scan photos.

"Aww, look, Gabe." She held out the photo to her husband who smiled warmly as he looked down at the image of my unborn baby.

"Perfect, so it must take after you, Bea."

I watched on as Seb flipped Gabe off while Carrie and I laughed at their juvenile banter.

"I'll get the beer," called Gabe to his friend who was already following him.

"Shame you girls are on soft drinks," teased Seb.

"Yeah, but you're going to need that beer to prepare for telling Charlotte she's not going to be the only baby in your life." Carrie laughed and was clearly teasing back, especially as Charlotte was totally on board with her parents having a new baby, but when I looked at Seb, he looked truly worried.

Chapter Forty-One

Seb

Charlotte sat on my lap with one arm draped around my neck. She really was the most delightful little girl and the love and adoration between us was mutual and reciprocal. I couldn't help but wonder what Imogen would have been like when I was with Charlotte, and honestly, I always hoped she'd be a lot like my niece.

She liked Bea and was happy to chat to her or play with her. She had spent time with Bea ever since Carrie had moved in so their relationship was independent of mine and hers and mine and Bea's, however, I had noticed that the little girl on my lap always managed to put a little space between me and my girlfriend.

"Charlotte, have you told Uncle Seb about what name you like for the baby?" Carrie asked with a very obvious smirk.

"Angel, you need to stop…it's not happening," said Gabe, confirming there was a reason for his wife's amusement.

Charlotte turned, maintaining her position in my lap and with excitement began to tell me. "I did like Henry, but Mummy said no because she doesn't like Henry's mummy."

Gabe laughed at Carrie being outed by their daughter. Maybe she hadn't fully thought out unleashing Charlotte's thoughts.

"Right," I said, still clueless as to where this was going.

"I don't like girl's names because I don't want us to have a girl, so I won't think of one," Charlotte told me with a pout."

"But if the baby is a girl," began Bea.

"I don't want it to be. We're going to send it back if it's a girl," Charlotte insisted.

"Sweetie, we can't send the baby back," Gabe told her looking concerned that this might be a real issue.

I decided to switch her attention back to names for the baby, a boy that she did want. "So, what would you like the baby to be named if he is a boy?"

"Uncle Seb," she replied and leaned in to kiss me.

I laughed loudly, more of a roar really. "Uncle Seb?"

"Yes, because you are funny and beautiful and I love you so much," she told me as she squeezed me tightly.

"I can't argue with that you beautiful baby girl."

She giggled, Carrie and Bea laughed, while Gabe shook his head.

"No chance," my old friend said.

"Maybe not the uncle bit," I said to Charlotte. "But Sebastian, Seb is a brilliant name."

"I told you," Charlotte said to her father and then turned to Carrie. "Please, can we call him Seb?"

"Daddy and I need to discuss names and there are lots more names for us to choose from."

"But I get to choose, don't I? I am the big sister."

Gabe looked across at his wife and gave her a cocky look that her wind up of him was backfiring now. "Sweetie, we can all choose one together once we know if the baby is a boy or girl and you can help us to decide but you can't choose on your own."

"Okay," she replied a little reluctantly but clearly knew this was the best option available to her.

"Speaking of babies," said Bea, and I knew where she was directing this conversation. I just wasn't sure how I felt to be embarking on it.

"Charlotte," I began, regaining her full attention.

She turned and smiled.

"You know that Mummy is having a baby and you're going to be the big sister?"

She nodded and smiled again, this time a little brighter and broader.

"Well, how would you feel about being a big cousin, too?" I gave myself a mental pat on the back for putting it out there in such a way that it played to Charlotte and her role being at the centre of this. Fuck knows what I would do if she decided she didn't fancy the job.

She frowned. "I don't have any cousins, do I?"

She did, but none she knew about or was in touch with.

Both Gabe and I shook our heads.

"Hmmm. So how do I become a cousin?"

"Well, you need an auntie or an uncle to have a baby and the baby would be your cousin and you would be the baby's cousin."

"Hmmm."

Her use of that little humming sound was making me seriously fucking nervous. How did this compact powerhouse of a four-year-old manage to cause such fear in me?

"I don't know many aunties or uncles, except you—"

She cut herself off and her face dropped. Immediately she removed herself from my lap and standing, turned to stare at me, accusingly.

I waited, we all waited. Sensing my nerves, Bea reached across and squeezed my hand, a move that wasn't missed by Charlotte who now glared at the interaction.

"What if I don't want a cousin?"

This was going downhill fast and I had no way of salvaging it. Nanny interrupted.

"That's not really your choice, sweetheart. If an uncle or an auntie decided to have a baby and they were really, really happy and excited about it, like we're excited about our baby, then we would be happy and excited for them."

She looked between Nanny and me and still didn't seem convinced. Gabe could see this too, so now he chipped in.

"If they were happy and we weren't, we might make them sad and we wouldn't want to do that, would we? You love Uncle Seb and would never want to make him sad, would you?"

Charlotte shook her head and stepped closer before climbing back into my lap. "Are you giving me a cousin, Uncle Seb?"

I nodded and braced myself for her reaction, not that I knew what it would be.

"Are you going to be my cousin's daddy?"

Again, I nodded.

"Hmmm…"

Fuck, there it was again.

"What about me? You always tell me how much you love me and how I am your favourite girl?"

I was saddened that she might ever think I would do anything other than love her but did smile when she cut Bea a look when she mentioned being my favourite girl.

"You will always be my favourite girl and I will never stop loving you." I meant every word. Charlotte was something to me that no other child, boy or girl could ever be. For all intents and purposes, she, along with Gabe had saved me.

"Okay," she looked back at Bea. "Are you going to be the mummy, like Mummy is?"

Bea grinned and nodded her head. "And I am really happy and excited too. I can't wait for us all to do things together; you, me, Mummy, Daddy, the babies and your Uncle Seb."

If I didn't think it would result in Charlotte lunging for my girlfriend I would have kissed and hugged her there and then for the way she'd put the emphasis on me belonging to Charlotte. For knowing that this little girl's life had changed almost beyond recognition in less than a year and she needed reassurances rather than chastisement. The truth was that at some point this little girl was going to have her world rocked by revelations about her birth mother so between us we needed to ensure that for now her world was solid, happy and full of love.

Charlotte turned on my lap so she was facing her parents, and as if they hadn't been there all along addressed them with her news. "I am going to be a big sister and a big cousin."

She grinned and crinkled her nose, looking like the cutest bundle of loveliness I had ever seen in my life.

I breathed a huge sigh of relief as I reached for my favourite girl to throw her around and make her laugh and squeal.

Chapter Forty-Two

Bea

It had been another couple of weeks since my scan and the little morning sickness I'd experienced seemed to be on the wane. Carrie was still suffering a couple of times a day, but all in all we were both healthy and enjoying our pregnancies.

Maurice had lined up a couple of possible replacements for me and was due to interview them but wanted me to join him in that. I was quite touched that he wanted my input at all.

I was meeting Carrie for lunch and we were both child free as Charlotte was doing a full day at nursery and Maurice had taken the children out for the day. Carrie had invited me to hers and as much as I enjoyed our meet ups in cafes it was nice to stay at home and relax and chat.

When I arrived at hers, she flung the door open and her belly seemed to have exploded since I'd last seen her, only a few days before.

"Wow," I said, unable to hide my smile.

"Don't say a word. My waist has abandoned me, and I may cry if I think about it much more."

"You look lovely." I hugged her warmly. "I think I might have bump envy."

We both laughed while Carrie pulled back and rubbed a hand across the swell of her belly. "Yeah, I won't really cry. I'm kind of loving having some physical evidence of a baby being there. I also think it helps to make if real for Charlotte. Plus, Gabe can't keep his hands off it."

I nodded and returned her grin, thinking that made perfect sense, even the bit about Gabe's hands, although he couldn't keep his hands off her anyway.

"And how are you and the daddy-to-be?" she asked with a giggle, already knowing that since he'd embraced impending fatherhood, Seb had gone into full daddy mode.

"Desperate to buy everything ever invented for a baby."

"Come on, let's go and eat lunch and we can bemoan our excited expectant fathers and their need to provide while we stuff our faces and nourish our babies."

I was on my second, or possibly third scone when Carrie asked about my living arrangements, as in, when was I going to move in with Seb? He'd asked several times and although I didn't doubt I would eventually, I was in no hurry.

"Bea, you must know that you can't say no forever."

I nodded. I did know that.

"Then what is the problem?"

"It scares me. What if he hates me being there or if he irritates me when he cuts his toenails in front of the TV?"

"Seb cuts his toenails in front of the TV?" She looked aghast.

I laughed at her horrified expression and clarified. "Not that I am aware of, but what if he does or something else I dislike?"

"And what if he doesn't? Or maybe he will irritate you in ways you're unaware of, and you him, but if you love each other and plan on making a future with your baby, you might have to try it."

"Yeah, I know. Having my own place is a big thing for me. I know my place isn't grand or anywhere near as nice as Seb's house, but it is mine. When I am there I feel as though I have achieved something and by giving it up it feels as though I am giving up a piece of me and my independence." There, I'd said it, admitted my fears.

"I get that, really I do. When Gabe and I hooked up properly I wasn't just risking a broken romance or being emotionally hurt. It was my job, my home and my feelings on the line. And if you remember it took me a while to officially move out from upstairs."

I looked across at her and although I already knew the

answer, I asked the question anyway. "No regrets?"

"No, not a single one. Look at me; I have a husband, a child, a baby on the way, I am loved like I didn't know existed and I have never been happier. The only drawback is that if we have loud sex there's a possibility of Charlotte hearing, whereas when I lived upstairs there wasn't."

I pulled a face and then we both laughed.

"Maybe I could try moving some stuff into Seb's and spending more time there and see how it goes."

"I think that's a very wise approach, and if you tell Seb what you've told me I am sure he will support you all the way."

"I hope so. Now, what the hell is with all the flowers still?" I gestured at the couple of vases of flowers on top of the nearby cupboard.

Carrie laughed. "They just won't die. They are the last ones from the dozens Gabe sent weeks ago when he pissed me off. He keeps filling the water up and they keep going."

I shook my head. "You've kissed and made up now though?"

"Yeah, kissed, shagged a dozen different ways, and made up."

We both giggled and then, as I thought of something that had been on my mind, I was glad again that we were pregnant together.

"Can I ask you something personal?"

Carrie nodded, reaching for another slice of lemon drizzle cake.

"Sex, is it different since being pregnant?"

She put her cake back down and sat back in her chair. "It is different as in Gabe is more careful with me and some of the positions I imagine will change as my belly grows."

"No, does it feel different? More intense?"

"Ah, yeah. I have found everything is a bit more sensitive and although I never had a problem getting there with Gabe, well, a single touch can have me soaring."

"I aim to please, Angel." Gabe appeared behind her and I felt my face grow warm as my embarrassment rose.

"And you certainly do, lover."

He leaned down and kissed her, laughing at her 'lover.' "You little minx." He kissed her again and for a second, I was sure they had forgotten I was there. "I thought I would work from home this afternoon and collect Charlotte while you put your feet up, both of you," he said with a smile in my direction.

"Thank you." Carrie looked so happy, especially when Gabe rubbed a hand over her bump. "Get Seb to pick you up from here. You can stay for dinner if you want."

I nodded and dropped Seb a text to that effect. I also added that I'd been thinking about us living together and wondered if we could talk about details.

<Whatever you want Princess. I just want you to be happy and safe. You, me and our baby. X>

I reread his message with a smile. Remembering seeing Carrie with Gabe months before and just now, I realised that I could have all of the things she had if I only allowed myself to, and I was going to.

Chapter Forty-Three

Seb

I saw Gabe as soon as I entered the bar. He sat on a bar stool eating peanuts and chatting with the staff behind the bar. He looked happy, relaxed, at ease with himself as well as life in general and he deserved to be. He had everything he'd ever wanted. Everything he once thought he'd found, we both had, but now, with Carrie, it truly was the real deal. And if he could recover from the past and find his nirvana, maybe I could. I just needed to allow myself to.

"Make mine a double," I said as I took the seat next to him.

"That bad?"

"Yup! Bea is currently taking over my house, which I'm happy about, but fuck me, I honestly do not care if my baked beans and spaghetti are mixed up in the cupboard."

Gabe laughed. "I feel you, mate. When I left, Carrie had plans to put Charlotte to bed and then, and I quote, was going to sort the bathroom towels out."

"What does that even mean?" I really was interested to know what it was about towels that needed sorting.

"Not a fucking clue, but I'm glad I'm not at home for it."

It was my turn to laugh now. "Do you suppose this is pregnancy related?"

"Wishful thinking there, we can but hope. Anyway, how you doing? You seem happy." Gabe smiled at me, warmly and genuinely.

"I can't lie, I am seriously happy which makes me smug as

176

fuck. I never thought I would find this again, and whilst I would do anything to bring Imogen back, I know that's not possible, but hope it might be as good the second time around."

Gabe nodded. "I totally get that. Not that I didn't love Alice, I did..."

I looked at my friend and could see how uncomfortable he was. He had loved my sister, been married to her, but he now loved Nanny, and why wouldn't he? She was everything he could ever want and more. I didn't want to be the reason for his discomfort because Nanny was his soulmate and as much as he and Alice might have loved each other, they weren't soulmates, of that, I was sure.

"Gabe, you don't have to explain it to me or feel obliged to understate you and Nanny because of me and Alice. I loved Alice and she was a good sister to me, but she was disturbed, badly, and always had been. You have never looked happier than you do with Nanny, and that thrills me."

"Impending parenthood is turning you into a pussy," he accused with a smile.

I flipped him off but couldn't deny what he was saying entirely. "Yeah, you and me both. When do you get to find out what sex the baby is?" I knew it was soon but was shit with dates.

"Next week." My friend grinned broadly.

"How's Charlotte? Still adamant that this baby is going back if it's a girl?"

"Yes, she is. So, although both Carrie and I would be happy with a boy or girl, we are hoping for the former."

I clinked my glass with his. "Then, here's to team blue."

"I'll drink to that. How about you? Do you fancy a blue or pink revelation?"

I sat in silence while my friend looked at me and waited for a response. Gabe and I didn't lie to each other, never had and I wasn't going to start now, but the truth was that I wasn't sure if I was ready to admit the thoughts in my head.

"Sorry. Let's have a change of topic, something that doesn't involve babies, pregnant women or the need to sort cupboards or towels."

"Thanks."

"Anytime."

"Maurice has appointed a new nanny. Bea said she's nice, a little older, but she was first choice for them both."

"That sounds good, especially for when Bea goes back to work."

"Hmmm."

Gabe laughed then frowned. "You don't sound too convinced by her going back to work."

I couldn't deny that my preference was for her staying at home with our baby rather than going to work to care for someone else's children. "I don't object to it in principal, but I prefer the idea of her being at home with the baby."

Gabe nodded, he got it, as I knew he would because he wouldn't want anyone else taking care of Charlotte and the baby. Indeed, Carrie had been the person he had entrusted Charlotte to, and it had taken him three years to agree to it.

"I will support whatever she wants though."

My friend laughed at that, loudly. "I'm almost convinced by that. Look, I get it, you'll support whatever she wants, but you'll support it easier if she chooses to stay at home with the baby. I suppose I've been lucky in that Charlotte went from being Carrie's job to being her daughter, so she never had to choose between work and family."

I couldn't deny what he was saying and almost envied the ease with which he had got his home life organised and ordered to his satisfaction. I had no plan as to what I could or should say but nobody was more surprised than me by the eight words that left my mouth. "The idea of a baby girl scares me."

Gabe ordered more drinks. "Okay."

"I really want this baby."

He smiled but said nothing.

"I am shitting myself that it might be a girl…I had a baby girl and I lost her."

"Is it that you're scared you won't love her as much as you did Imogen, or do you feel guilty that you might find yourself thinking about Imogen less?"

They were both good questions and both of them were in my

head, but it was more than that for me. "Loving Imogen was the easiest thing I ever did, the most natural thing and entirely unconditional. Losing her was the hardest and most painful thing I've experienced."

He reached across and patted my arm. He'd been there and lived it with me, so he knew exactly what I was saying.

"The idea of replacing Imogen makes me feel like the biggest shit in the world. She was my baby and if I can love another daughter as much or think about her less then what does that say about how much she meant to me? What does it say about me?"

Gabe remained silent and simply looked at me. His silence and simple glance said that we both knew that was bollocks. Not that I was thinking it, but logically I could rationalise that I was skirting around the real issue.

"I am sure I will love her or him as much as I did Imogen. I'm unsure if that immediate rush will be there, but I don't doubt my love. What if I lose another baby, Gabe? I wouldn't survive it, not again. I barely survived it the first time." There, it was out. I'd admitted my greatest fear to the one person who totally understood what I had been through and just how low I had been.

"Nobody can guarantee loss or lack of it, but statistically it is most unlikely, you know that. I do know how hard it is to leave yourself open to that possibility though. When everything happened and it was just me and Charlotte, I vowed that it was the two of us forever. I was never falling in love again, never mind getting married and there was no way I'd have more children. You know I dated, kind of, but it was never more than casual, and then I met Carrie."

"Ah, Nanny." I smiled at my friend's pathetically happy and dopey smile.

"Yes, Carrie. Nothing prepared me for her, nothing in my past could have equipped me with the skills to contend with what she brought to my life. She put me on my arse and before I knew it, I was in deep. When we got married, I had it all and although I hadn't ruled out having children with Carrie, we hadn't really discussed it."

I arched a brow, my surprise clear.

"I know. She assumed we would have children and I hadn't given it much real thought. We talked about it in principle, the idea of it, but neither of us discussed a time frame and I assumed that meant Carrie was in no hurry. When she sprung it on me after we married, I was shocked and scared. Charlotte had been my everything for most of her life, at the expense of everything else, so the idea of opening up and doing it again…well, I too doubted my ability to do it with the same love and enthusiasm, but when Carrie told me she was pregnant, my doubts left me, as I think yours will when Junior puts in an appearance."

"Thank you."

No further words were needed. My friend, who was so much more than that, he understood me like nobody else, and I knew him.

"Right, let me get a round in and then we can talk rugby, look at the length of that woman's legs, and then I really need to discuss pregnancy porn."

"Absolutely, unless my wife asks and then we only talked rugby."

"Who's the pussy now?"

Chapter Forty-Four

Bea

"You okay?" I looked across at Seb as he entered the bedroom where I had almost finished getting dressed.

"I would be if Nanny would stop busting my balls every time I go near her or her bloody boxes."

I laughed. Today, we were doing a gender reveal party and neither Seb nor I knew the sex of our baby. We had given Carrie a sealed envelope with that information in and left the rest to her. We were having a small gathering in our garden and my friend was busy organising everything, including Seb it would seem.

"Princess, it's not funny…she has just sent me indoors like a child and she's in my house."

His pout made me laugh again. I joined him, sitting on the bed and rested my head on his shoulder at the same time that I pulled his hand onto my unmistakable baby bump.

"She is quite fearsome."

Seb laughed now. "Understatement of the year."

"Could be worse, you could be Gabe."

He laughed again. "Yeah, but he loves it, he loves her."

"Yeah, and she wants this to be perfect because she loves us, and she loves our baby. I for one can't think of anyone better to have in the corner of loving and looking out for him or her, can you?"

He thought for a moment. "No, I can't. Woe betide anyone who crosses Nanny when she's in protective mode."

"Exactly. You should ask her about the little boy who's been pulling Charlotte's hair."

"I will, and if she hasn't put a stop to it, I will go and sort him out myself."

I looked up at Seb and adjusted my position so I sat astride him. "You and Carrie aren't so different, you know, and I love that you are so protective."

He pushed some loose hair behind my ear. "I love you."

I would never tire of hearing him telling me that he loved me, ever. We didn't overuse it or utter it so frequently it was at risk of becoming a token or somehow throwaway.

"I love you, too."

Seb slipped a hand around my neck until he was cupping the back of my head and pulling me closer. Our lips touched and instinctively I pulled him closer still, my hands wrapped around him and my thighs tightened their grip. Before anything else registered, we were rolling until I found myself lying on my back on the bed with Seb over me, his body between my legs.

The sound of the door being knocked and then opened was followed by Carrie's voice. "What the bloody hell! I need you both outside in five minutes so if you can finish up here in that time, great, otherwise you'll need to cut it short."

We both stared at her as she simply turned her back and left. Seb rolled onto his back next to me and we both began to laugh. We laughed even louder when we heard her speak to Gabe and muttered something about *I may have given your friend blue balls*. Seb could barely breathe when he heard his friend shout back something about his being the only blue balls she should be responsible for.

"Later, when it's just the two of us and we have disagreed on some more names, we will pick this up." Seb leaned over and kissed the tip of my nose.

"I look forward to it and we can rule out half of the names we can't agree on once we know whether we are team pink or team blue."

He grinned but he looked a little nervous at finding out the sex of our baby and I got it. A girl would make him remember Imogen. I tried to support his nerves but if our baby was a girl there was nothing we could do about it and I would be thrilled.

Just a few nights ago when we had been discussing names, I had suggested Imogen and he lost his shit slightly. I hadn't meant as a first name but as a middle name to honour his first child and somehow incorporate her into our family. It was after that when I realised how much of a struggle the idea of another girl was for him.

"I'm going to find Gabe and tell him what a nightmare his wife is." He got to his feet and reached down to help me sit back up. "I will see you out there." He landed another kiss, to my lips this time, and left me to put on some flip-flops with the brightly patterned maxi-dress I wore.

I stifled a loud and raucous laugh when I heard Gabe ask Seb, "Do you want to tell me what you, my wife and your blue balls have been up to?"

I couldn't contain my amusement when I heard my boyfriend's reply. "That's between me, her and my blue balls, but you know there's always been a spark between me and Nanny."

"Fuck off, dickhead!" Gabe's reply coincided with me leaving the bedroom in time to see him flip off Seb.

"Come on then, boys, before Carrie comes a hunting."

****

The garden looked amazing; there were dozens of banners in pink and blue, tables with tablecloths covered in ducks, balloons, rabbits and ribbons and the assembled guests sat nearby. Maurice was manning the barbecue while his new nanny, Flora, stood nearby, chatting and laughing with him while the children played nearby. In the centre of the garden was a huge white box with a lid on it.

Charlotte saw us all first and with a squeal rushed towards us, ambushing Seb who immediately picked her up.

"Uncle Seb, can we find out what the baby is now?"

I laughed at her impatience. It was a good job Carrie hadn't told the little girl the gender of our baby or it wouldn't have remained a secret for long. Charlotte was obsessed with the sex of my baby and her mother's. Gabe and Carrie hadn't done the gender reveal thing as we were. They had gone for their scan and kept it to themselves for a few days and then they had told

Charlotte that the baby had sent her a gift to tell her whether it was a baby brother or sister. Gabe had recorded the moment on his phone, and it had been quite moving to see the little girl open a gift box containing a beautiful teddy bear wearing a t-shirt that said from your baby brother. The little girl had laughed, then cried and hugged her parents, both of whom were crying by the end of it and now it was my turn to find out whether I was waiting to welcome a boy or a girl.

Chapter Forty-Five

Seb

"You all set?" Gabe had flung an arm around my shoulder after we'd discussed his wife's roll in my blue balls.

"Yeah, I am actually." I was and I felt calmer than I had about the whole thing. I was still hoping for a boy, for the sake of ease, but if it wasn't, I'd be okay.

He patted my back and led me outside. We had invited a few friends and Christine and Noel were there. I loved them, they were my surrogate parents and I hoped would fill the role of grandparents to my baby, whether it was a boy or a girl. I was glad we had chosen to find out the sex of the baby but was beginning to wish we'd taken a leaf out of Gabe and Nanny's book and done so privately. I knew I thought I'd be okay if the baby was a girl, and I would be, but I was still nervous and now with an audience, I would need to ensure that I didn't look anything that resembled disappointed. I wouldn't be. I had accepted that it was my baby, as Imogen had been regardless of gender. That's not to say I wasn't still nervous or fearful that another girl wouldn't be overwhelming. I might just need a moment and now that moment was potentially going to be with onlookers.

Charlotte ambushed me and was desperate to find out whether she got the baby boy or girl cousin. Fuck me, I hadn't even considered that! If this baby was a girl, not only would I have to deal with my own feelings, I was going to have a disappointed Charlotte. And whilst I would do my best to mask any negative thoughts, she would not.

With my beautiful niece in my arms and her desire to connect with my baby, I was ready. "Let's do it then my beautiful girl."

She clapped, making everyone laugh. "Shall I help you?"

I was all ready to say yes, but Nanny intervened.

"Why don't we let Bea and Uncle Seb do this together?" She'd said it as a question but was already taking her from me.

I could hear the first of Charlotte's 'but Mummy' when Bea came along side me.

"Are you ready to do this, Daddy?"

I stared down at her and laughed. "Princess, the daddy thing is not my usual kink, but if you want to try it later, I'm game, but for now, maybe keep it to yourself."

Bea laughed, and Nanny, who stood nearby, rolled her eyes. Gabe stood next to her and whispered something in her ear that made her flush. I couldn't focus on sex or whatever kinky thing they were into right now...I had a baby's gender to reveal, my baby.

"Come on then, let's do it." I took Bea's hand and led her to the huge cardboard box in the middle of the garden.

"Stand behind it," bellowed Nanny who had Gabe on standby to record this moment, while Christine was taking photos.

We moved as instructed while she shouted further orders to Gabe and Christine and then she turned back to us.

"After three...one, two, three..."

Bea and I took one side of the lid each to reveal a sea of white balloons that began to rise. We watched as one after another they soared before our eyes before lifting the biggest and final balloon in the shape of a baby's bottle. A giant foil shaped bottle full of helium in blue.

"It's blue!" I cried with actual tears escaping my eyes. When I looked at Bea, she was crying too. "It's a boy," I said, my voice quivering. "We're having a boy." If somebody didn't confirm this soon, I was going to drown in my own words.

"Congratulations." Gabe was the first to approach me and confirm that I was going to be a father to a boy, as he was.

Nanny was crying and cursing hormones as she engulfed Bea with a hug, still holding Charlotte over her baby bump who was cheering and telling everyone she was going to have a baby brother and a baby cousin.

I reached for Bea, pulled her to me and held her tightly, half hoisting her up in my arms while we both laughed and cried. This had to be one of those perfect moments that stayed with you a whole lifetime.

With the cat out of the bag, or at least the balloon out of the box, I relaxed and enjoyed the whole afternoon; we ate, laughed and celebrated our baby boy's existence. When we cut the cake, we found the inside was blue. Nanny removed Charlotte's t-shirt to reveal another one underneath that had the image from one of our scan photos on it with the words, in blue, 'have you met my cousin?' Nanny really had done an amazing job.

****

Once everyone had gone home, leaving just me and Bea, we lay on the sofa together, her stroking my face and me stroking her belly.

"I have never been this happy before," I told her, and it was true. I couldn't remember ever feeling this happy, without any reservation or something lurking in the background.

She leaned up and cupping my face, gently pulled my lips to hers to kiss me. "Me neither. I didn't even think this degree of happy existed."

"It does for us, and our boy, our family."

She teared up at my sappy words, but it was all true.

"You know we need to think of a name for him now."

I shook my head. "We have another three and a half months left. But at least we can never discuss names like Primrose or Gardenia, or whatever the fuck those other ridiculous names were."

She laughed. "Gardenia? Where did that come from? I said I liked Primrose or Jasmine."

"Yeah, well, I don't and they're all flowers, aren't they?"

She kissed me again. "And now we don't have to because our baby is a boy."

"Yes, he is." I pulled her in closer and kissed her, not the loving, chaste kisses she'd bestowed on me, but a harder, deeper kiss that saw her wrapping her arms and legs around me as my tongue danced with hers.

When we came up for breath her eyes were wide and glazed, she looked stoned on just a kiss. God, I loved this woman and the depth of her love, want and desire for me blew me away every time I saw it.

"What about Orlando?"

I was confused by her question. "I didn't realise you were into theme parks or Disney."

She laughed loudly at my response and misunderstanding. "I meant as a name, not a holiday."

"No fucking chance."

"Bryson?"

"No."

"Crew?"

"What the fuck is the matter with you? Do you want the shit kicking out of our boy on a daily basis?" I had no clue where these ridiculous names were coming from and then she laughed, at me. "Ah, you're taking the piss?"

She shrugged and bit her lip.

I rubbed her belly, then leaned down and kissed it before addressing my son. 'My son.' That was weird, overwhelming, and fucking amazing at the same time. "Mummy is going to find herself in all kinds of trouble if she keeps winding Daddy up like this."

"Barrington," she called out, interrupting my talk with my boy.

"Oh, yes she is, son. She is going to find herself on all fours getting fucked hard and maybe having her arse spanked if she utters another ridiculous name tonight."

"Augustus," she called immediately.

I kissed her belly again. "Sorry about this my boy, but Mummy needs taking to task, so we'll pick up our guy talk later." I crawled back up her body. "Oh dear, Princess, you and I should probably take this somewhere more comfortable."

Her breathing hitched and her chest was rising and falling rapidly. She nodded and licked her lips, making them even more appealing than they usually were.

"Take me to bed, Seb."

"You want to be on all fours getting fucked hard?"

She nodded and the flush on her cheeks spread down her neck and chest.

"And do you need your arse spanking a little?"

She nodded again and clenched her thighs.

"Then let's go to bed."

I helped Bea to her feet and walked behind her as she went upstairs and was unable to hide the smug smile on my face. I hadn't been wrong earlier when I'd thought I had never been happier, I hadn't.

Chapter Forty-Six

Bea

Seb was handling me like a precious artefact that might break at any moment as he lay me on the bed having already stripped me of my clothes. He lay alongside me and kissed me. The gentleness of his kiss was unexpected after his words downstairs but brought with it a different type of passion. This wasn't frantic and bang you against a wall passion, but loving, tender and caring. The way he gently stroked his fingers over my skin, the softness of his kiss and the look of love in his eyes told me just how much me and our baby meant to him, how happy he was and how much he needed me.

I reached up and attempted to pull him closer at the same time as putting zero space between us, hoping to facilitate the physical closeness and intimacy we both craved. Unfortunately, my expanding belly was beginning to get in the way.

"We might need to rethink this, Princess."

"You could be right there, babe."

"You can get on your hands and knees, or we can spoon or you can climb on top...your choice." He grinned, happy for any or all of the above.

"How about you lie back and think of England and I'll do the hard work?"

"Whatever you want. I am, after all, in favour of equal rights."

I laughed at his cheeky smirk and once he was on his back, I moved to straddle him. "That all fours suggestion, though...

maybe we could come back to it."

"Not a problem. Now get yourself here."

He pulled me down to him then kissed me. As the kiss deepened, he reached for my behind and cupped it, enabling me to move so that his erection was poised at my entrance.

Slowly, I inched down his length easily due to the moisture of my arousal, but still, my body needed a little time to adjust to the invasion. Once I had him fully encased, I broke our kiss and leaned back into a sitting position. My arms naturally came to rest at my sides so my hands gripped his hips and arse cheeks

I stared down at him, emotionally moved to fully realise he was mine, completely. I hadn't realised how moved until he reached up and brushed a couple of stray tears from my face.

"Hey, you okay?" He looked concerned.

"Yes, totally. I just love you, so much."

He smiled. "Me too, more than I think is legal in some countries."

It was my turn to laugh at him now.

"Do you want to spoon and let me make love to you?"

I felt my emotions rising again with that offer of him wanting to take care of me and my emotional state. "No." I immediately began to move and as I did so, Seb placed his hands on my hips, encouraging and supporting my movements and efforts.

It was only a matter of a few minutes before ripples of pleasure began to spread through my body. I was close.

"Fuck, yes," Seb called as his grip on my hips tightened.

I continued to move, up and down, squeezing all of my internal muscles around his length that was beginning to twitch.

"Come on, Princess," he hissed from between gritted teeth while his hands moved to my breasts that he cupped then stroked until he reached my nipples that he squeezed firmly. That was the final touch I needed to reach my release.

In a flurry of cries, shouts and more erratic thrusts, I came hard. Hard enough that I took Seb there with me. He pulled my face to his and proceeded to kiss me until his hips and mine stilled.

"You might have to give me half an hour if you still fancy being on all fours."

I laughed as I dismounted and rolled onto my side, allowing Seb to spoon me.

"I might need to take a rain check on that," I replied as I let out a long, loud yawn.

"No problem. Sleep." He kissed the back of my neck and shoulders as a peaceful and contented sleep encompassed us both.

Chapter Forty-Seven

Seb

<u>Three Months Later</u>

"Are you sure?" I asked, doubting whether she was or not

Bea glared at me and threw a pillow in my direction. "What do you think?" Her question coincided with her doubling over in pain.

I avoided pointing out that this was the third time she'd been sure she was in labour, both previous times resulting in us enduring a wasted trip to the hospital.

"Shit!" She hissed that one word through tightly gritted teeth.

"Okay, okay." I grabbed my phone and with her following behind me we made our way downstairs.

With my car keys in my pocket, I reached for Bea's hand and led her to the car where we'd left her hospital bags.

Her contractions were well spaced out, so I was able to take things steady and in between huffs and puffs we chatted.

"Seb, I'm scared. It's early."

"Only by three weeks so I am sure he'll be just fine."

She nodded, but I wasn't even sure that three and a bit weeks early truly qualified as premature.

I laughed as I took her hand in mine when we pulled up on the hospital car park. "Nanny is going to be seriously pissed with you if our baby arrives before hers."

Bea let out a slightly sinister sounding cackle, mainly because she knew what I was saying was true. Our friends' baby was now almost two weeks overdue and his mother was beyond ready for her pregnancy to end.

"Do not call Gabe until the baby is here," she warned.

"No problem. I don't want to be on Nanny's shit list, thank you very much."

I leaned across to the passenger seat and kissed her lips gently. Then I got out and rounded the car to open her door, having already grabbed her bags. With an outstretched hand I helped her to stand as another contraction struck. She squeezed my hand tight enough to cut off the circulation or possibly break small bones, but I felt it wise not to complain at this point in time as she was likely to pass an actual person in the next twelve hours or so.

"Let's go and get ourselves a baby, Princess."

She smiled up at me and I was momentarily blown away, as I always was at the realisation that she was mine and together we had made this perfect life that we both already adored.

****

"Is this a joke?" Bea's question had no humour in it, nor laughter.

"You're doing amazing," I told her, hoping to lift her disappointment.

"I'd be doing amazing if I was eight or nine centimetres, not two."

The midwife looked across and smiled.

"Hey, you are giving life to our baby...you are amazing, and you are two centimetres closer to holding our baby than you've ever been."

She smiled up at me, a few tears shining in her eyes. "You have to be nice to me."

I shook my head. "I don't, but I choose to. Now, let's get you walking around and evicting our boy."

We passed the next few hours, walking around, bouncing on a giant ball, her not me, chatting and laughing as well as playing games against each other on our phones in an attempt to make the progression of Bea's labour as stress free as possible. The length and strength of the contractions were becoming more intense and my words of encouragement were becoming, not only less effective, but more of an irritant to my girlfriend.

Bea was six centimetres a couple of hours later. I had been sent to the shop in the hospital for some boiled sweets. I don't even think she wanted them, but it was an excuse to get rid of me for a little while. It was an opportunity I happily accepted as I was running out of ways to entertain her rather than piss her off.

With sweets, crisps and drinks bought, as well as a cuddly blue bunny, I made my way back up to the delivery suite. I was about to turn the corner into the corridor where Bea was when I heard a familiar voice. Gabe. I spun back and found my friend in a waiting area on his phone.

"Yes, sweetheart. I love you, too, and I will see you real soon."

He hung up and looked ecstatic.

"And what brings you here."

He jumped and turned fully to grin in my direction. "My pregnant wife is what brought me here and my no longer pregnant wife and son are still keeping me here."

His tears were not a surprise, mine however, shocked me. I rushed over to him and engulfed him in my arms, hugging him tightly.

"Congratulations. I am so happy for you. Have you got a photo of him? Please tell me he looks like Nanny and not your ugly mug."

He laughed but pulled back from me to open his photos. "Hang on. I have a better idea."

Gabe put his phone away and pulled me with him, coming to a standstill as he reached an identical door to the one I had left Bea behind. Before it registered, I had followed him in and was greeted by the sight of Nanny sitting up in bed, cradling a baby.

"You look bloody amazing, Nanny," I told her and meant it. She looked a little tired, slightly jaded, but she did look amazing, considering.

"Come and say hello." She grinned and leaned down to the baby. "This is Uncle Seb."

As I reached the bedside, she offered him up to me. I put the sweets and bunny down.

I took the beautiful, pink and wrinkly bundle and began to cry again. He was perfect and did look a lot like Nanny, but also like Gabe. When I looked back to the new mother, she was crying too and also cracking into my sweets.

She picked up the bunny and held it up to the baby. "Look what Uncle Seb has brought you."

Shit! She was eating sweets she thought were hers and had taken possession of my baby's bunny for her son. I figured I could buy more sweets and another bunny.

"I can't believe you got here so quickly," Nanny said. "He was only born about twenty minutes ago."

"What? Shit, I have to go."

I thrust the baby back towards his mother and began to rush to the door.

"Seb," Gabe called to me, concern in his voice. "Are you okay?"

"Yeah." I spun back to face them both. "Bea is in labour. Down the corridor."

Gabe opened the door before me and was preparing to push me out.

"I will be back. I'll bring my son to meet..." I had no clue what the baby was called.

"Sebastian," Carrie said to me.

"What?" I needed to get back to Bea and not stand here answering questions.

"Sebastian," she called again.

"What?" I was getting tetchy and was ready to walk out.

She laughed. I didn't.

"My son is called Sebastian, after his uncle."

I was stunned.

"And hopefully his godfather too," Gabe added, knocking the wind out of my sails.

"I need to go." I told them both.

"Here you are!" The midwife who was now standing in the doorway a little out of breath, grabbed my arm. "Your girlfriend is going to have this baby without you if you don't get yourself back in there."

Shit! This really was it.

Chapter Forty-Eight

Bea

I'd sent Seb to go for a walk, grab a drink or some sweets or something, anything. Anything that put a little space between us. He had been amazing, supportive and encouraging, but as my labour intensified and the contractions got worse, I wanted more and more to punch him, so this was a better option. Having said all of that, I hadn't expected him to be gone quite so long. I had been in labour about twelve hours and I was tired. I just wanted this over and done with and it felt as though I was about to get my wish.

"I think I want to push."

The midwife looked back at me and smiled. "I doubt you're quite ready, but let's check."

I swear that in the last twelve hours there had been more people up close and personal with my vagina than ever before.

"Ooh, you are very close. I'd say another centimetre and you will be done."

She made me sound like a Christmas turkey, but at this point I was beyond being offended. While she began to gather things, I wondered where Seb was.

"My boyfriend," I managed to mutter between contractions.

"Yeah, he's going to miss the action if he doesn't come back soon." She laughed, but seeing my horror at that happening she added, "Let's find him, eh?"

She stuck her head into the corridor and found her colleague who she left with me while she hunted Seb down, I hoped. It was only a few minutes later that she reappeared with my wayward boyfriend.

"Sorry, Princess, I found Gabe and Nanny here. Gabe, Nanny and baby Sebastian."

He looked so proud that I almost forgot about the wave of cramping that was knocking me off my feet. His best friend had called his son after him and he couldn't have been happier. Neither could I. We had ruled out having a Sebastian junior and whilst Seb was on board with it, I knew he was still slightly disappointed.

"Are they okay?"

"Perfect."

I screamed out as an undeniable urge to push and bear down washed over me.

The midwife stood between us. "Shall we get this baby out then?"

With some help, I got myself into a weird position, kneeling on the bed and gripping the head of it as though my life depended on it. Seb stood near my head and urged me on as he rubbed my back and held my hand. The midwife barked orders at me, orders I was happy to follow if it meant my baby would be here and these bloody contractions would end.

"And push," she said.

"Push," repeated Seb.

Seb repeated every one of her orders, push, pant, whatever and after the fifth or sixth time, I'd had enough. "Will you stop telling me what to bloody do. She is telling me, so I don't need you to, and the last time I checked you weren't a sodding vagina specialist."

His face broke into a huge grin, but I was in no mood for that or whatever smart arse comment I didn't doubt was poised on the tip of his tongue.

"Don't, just bloody don't."

He looked sheepish. "I was only trying to help."

I felt sorry for him and his lost schoolboy expression until an almighty contraction washed over me. "Yeah, well, unless you can pass a melon through your genitals for me, me and my fairy do not need your assistance."

He lost all control now and laughed. "Did you just call your vagina a fairy?"

"Fuck off, Seb!" I sprayed a very unattractive string of spit as the midwife gave another 'big push' instruction.

I did and then, with Seb taking a step down the bed, the sound of my baby's cry sounded around the room, his cry, then Seb's and mine.

Everything seemed to happen in a slow-motion blur. The baby cried and as I looked over my shoulder he was held aloft. Seb was sobbing as he looked at our son. He cut the cord and as I was helped into a more comfortable position the baby was offered to me. Seb still cried but never once took his eyes off our boy.

"Are you okay?" I asked, genuine concern seeping through.

He nodded but said nothing as the baby was offered to me. Seb still seemed to be struggling for words.

"You hold him first." I smiled at the midwife who nodded and offered the baby to Seb who had taken the seat next to the bed.

I watched on as my son received his first cuddle from his daddy.

"He looks like you," I told him, tears running down my cheeks and emotion filling my voice.

And then the penny dropped. Seb held the baby, rocked him and attempted to offer him some soothing words. The baby curled into his father's embrace and settled in the safety of his arms. Seb looked up at me and then back down at his son, tears still falling, his and mine.

"He looks like Imogen."

I nodded, unsure whether this was going to make becoming a father for the second time easier or harder for Seb.

"It's like I get another chance at fatherhood, but I get a piece of my baby girl back too."

More tears followed, but they were happy tears, only happy tears.

The last hour had been spent gazing down at the perfect baby boy lying in my arms after we'd both stemmed the flow of our tears. Both Seb and I were in absolute awe. Neither of us had the words to describe this moment, so we didn't even try.

Seb's text alert sounded. "Gabe," he explained. "Are we going to them or are they coming here?"

I shrugged. "Either. Are you sure we're allowed to?"

Before he could answer, a midwife and porter appeared to take me and Freddie, the baby, up to the ward where I'd be in a small bay with other new mums and their babies. Freddie was put back into the plastic bowl that would be his bed tonight and we were both wheeled to the lift.

As we entered the ward, we were taken to a bay to find only one of the four beds was currently occupied, by Carrie. Charlotte propelled herself across the space to Seb, who immediately picked her up.

"Well, what brings you here?" he asked her as he kissed her.

"My baby. His name is Sebastian like you." She sounded surprised and startled by that fact.

"Wow! He is so lucky to have such an amazing name. And is your baby brother as gorgeous as you?"

Charlotte laughed and pulled Seb in for another hug.

"I know, that was a really silly question, wasn't it? Because nobody could ever be as gorgeous as you, could they?"

She squeezed him tighter.

"How about you come and meet your baby cousin as you've met your brother."

I was settled in bed and watched on as Seb sat Charlotte in the chair and picked Freddie up.

"This is Freddie, and Freddie, this is your amazing big cousin, Charlotte."

"Hello, Freddie," she whispered to him.

Gabe and Carrie came over and joined us with baby Sebastian.

"Sebastian is really called Sebastian Christopher," Charlotte told us.

"And Freddie is really called Freddie Gabriel."

The little girl giggled. "So, my baby has your name and your baby has Daddy's name."

"Yes, they do." Seb beamed.

"And they have the same birthday," Charlotte seemed to realise. "Like twins."

"Kind of," said Carrie. "But with different mummies and daddies."

"Unless...Nanny," Seb said with a mischievous grin and a cheeky wink at his inference about baby Seb being the result of some torrid encounter he and Carrie had shared.

Carrie laughed. "Er, no."

Gabe flipped him off with a grin of his own and reverted conversation back to our children's shared birthday. "Brother from another mother."

Seb laughed. "Twin from another quim."

We all laughed now, although Gabe did quickly reach over and cover his daughter's ears. Not quickly enough.

"What's a quim?"

"Right, we need to go home," Gabe told Charlotte.

With everybody ready to go home, Carrie walked Gabe and Charlotte off the ward while Seb hung back with me and Freddie.

"Thank you. I never knew I could be this happy again and it is all down to you," he told me.

I sniffed back tears. "My pleasure. There is nobody in this world that deserves to be this happy and nobody else I want to make happy."

He leaned in and kissed me gently on the lips. "Tell me we will always try our hardest to make each other happy, no matter what."

"We will." I ran my hand across his cheek.

"Promise."

I raised my hand and extended my little finger. "Pinky promise."

With his forehead resting against mine and our son sleeping in my arms between us, he linked his own pinky with mine and we shook them and together we swore it.

"Pinky promise."

THE END

Keep reading to discover the steamy standalone novel,
Disaster-in-Waiting

About the Author

Elle M Thomas was born in the north of England and raised near Birmingham, UK where she still lives with her family. She works in local education and writes in her spare time with dreams of becoming a full-time writer.

Whilst still at school, and with a love of writing slightly risqué tales of love and romance one of her teachers told her that she could be the next Harrold Robins. Elle didn't act on those words for many years. In February 2017, with her first book completed and a dozen others unfinished, she finally took the plunge and self-published the steamy romance, Disaster-in-Waiting.

Elle describes her books as stories filled with chemistry, sensuality, love and sex that she always wanted to read and her characters as three dimensional and flawed.

Social media links for Elle M Thomas:

Twitter – Elle M Thomas Author

Facebook – Elle M Thomas and Elle's Belles

Instagram – authorellemthomas

Goodreads – Elle M. Thomas

Have you read Disaster-in-Waiting by Elle M Thomas?

Disaster-in-Waiting

Chapter One

My friends, the ones I had at that point warned me that I was marrying my dad and I had no issue with that, none at all. Michael was older than me, by thirty years, but when I was twenty-three he seemed awfully exotic with his greater knowledge and experience of, well, everything. He represented all the positives of a good dad in my mind; he was caring, protective, and considerate of my needs and wants, and he offered me security and safety, although like an overindulgent father he did spoil me, showering me with gifts and material possessions. I smiled with a still disbelieving shake of my head as I remembered how he had once bought me a new car because my old car, which was less than a year old was dirty. But here I was almost six years later married to my dad, or at least a dad, a man who played golf, often, read, a lot and not even works of fiction, big books on real life, history, geography, architecture, things I had no interest in. That was fine though. He had no issues with my interests, not that I had many, so I reciprocated.

My issue was sex, or lack thereof. If memory served me right, which it did, it had been six months since he'd touched me intimately and another six months since we'd had sex, real sex and at twenty-eight I wanted sex. Needed it. Craved it. After a few health scares after hitting fifty-five Michael had lost confidence and stamina so he'd distanced himself from me physically and as much as I wanted my needs fulfilling I didn't feel able to complain. Especially not as I knew how guilty my husband felt about his inability to satisfy my most basic needs.

He had been my boss, not my immediate boss, but my ultimate boss. He had owned the whole company I'd worked for, Stanton Industries, not that I understood what the business was, not really. I worked as a secretary for a middle manager in accounts on the seventh floor and Michael ran the whole shebang from his floor, the top floor, the twentieth where he occupied a corner office that looked out across the whole city. I didn't really know that when I was plain old Eloise Ross, although I was still Eloise Ross at work, having resisted the temptation to become Mrs Stanton in all areas of my life. Today I was to return there as P.A. to the new CEO having left my post there after marrying five years ago. I had been desperate to gain promotions and recognition in my own right, not for being married to the boss, which I'd done. Michael was no longer the boss, not since the downturn in his health when he'd made the decision to sell the company to a bigger conglomerate, Miller Industries.

"Darling, I've made you some tea. We don't want you to be late on your first day, do we?"

I smiled at my husband's kindness as I gave myself a final once over, dressed professionally in a black pencil skirt and a white silk blouse. I had opted for tights so I wouldn't be worrying all day that I was flashing stocking tops at my new boss, Denton Miller Snr who I had yet to meet in person. Along with commendations from my husband and a few webcam and Skype conversations I had decided that he was a boss I would enjoy working for.

Denton was of a similar age to Michael, but unlike my husband he had been married for thirty odd years to his teenage sweetheart and was living the American dream with his main home in California but numerous other residences around the world, seemingly in the cities that housed the offices of his vast business empire. Michael, by contrast had been married three times before me and I was the only wife not to have given him a child. Although sex would be required for a baby meaning that I was only a stepmother to four; two girls from wife number one, both older than me by a year and two years. His sons were aged twenty and fourteen with wives two and three respectively. God, I was like his middle child I realised with a smile, a smile that evaporated as I remembered I was also a step-nanny to three children under five and then he called me again.

"El, come on, Denton is a stickler for punctuality," he reminded me for the hundredth time causing me to bristle slightly.

"Yes, I know. I'm coming!" I screeched slipping black heeled shoes onto my feet but Michael laughed, annoying me further.

"If I was a jealous man those claims might offend me Mrs Stanton," he added as I appeared before him in the kitchen where my tea was waiting for me.

"What?" I asked impatiently, confused by his words.

"You shouted, *I'm coming.*"

Unsure how to react and thinking that if I did I might say something to open the can of worms that represented our lack of a sex life, I simply accepted the cup of tea and killed another ten minutes or so before dropping a kiss to Michael's head as I left the house.

Upon entering my former place of employment that was now my current place of employment I noted that very little appeared to have changed, except for the new signage.

"Hey there stranger," called the receptionist as I arrived on my new floor, my husband's old floor.

I spun to find a former colleague and friend, Maya, looking back at me with a grin spread across her face.

"What the bloody hell are you doing here?" I asked as I hugged the other woman, glad to find a friendly face. "Michael never mentioned you were back here."

"First day, babe. You remember I went to Provence with Aaron?"

I nodded, remembering her leaving a couple of years before with her boyfriend who had also worked for Michael but after his divorce was finalised decided to travel.

"Yeah, well that was great for a while, right up to the point where I found Aaron was indulging in some serious online shenanigans."

"No way!"

"Way babe. So, I packed up, after paying the astronomical internet bill. My oldest sister still works here, in H.R. so she offered to put my C.V. forward and here I am, receptionist for the exec floor and I believe you are Mr Miller's P.A.?"

"Yes, first day too."

"So, you and Mr Stanton..."

I could see that what Maya really wanted to ask was, 'are you still married to the old man?'

"Michael is at home."

"Ah," she replied dropping her glance to my narrow gold wedding ring. "I heard he'd been unwell."

"Yes," I confirmed. "He had some heart trouble that required surgery, but he's on the mend," I added with a smile that not even I was convinced by. "Look, I should go, apparently my new boss doesn't like lateness."

"Okay, later, we'll catch up."

At ten o'clock I wondered if Mr Miller was one of those, 'do as I say, not as I do' bosses because he was a no show and I was over an hour and a half into my day. I considered calling Michael to ask him if I should be concerned, but decided against it. Another hour and then I would attempt to contact Denton Miller.

Another hour came and went, however as I was engrossed in a stationery delivery I was unaware of anything that wasn't made of paper until it was almost one o'clock when Maya appeared in my doorway.

"Do you want to grab lunch?" she asked as I stood up and faced her, still flushed from my exertion unpacking new paperwork.

"You'd have thought that such a forward thinking company would rely on electronic copies of this shit," I observed, opening yet another box of compliment slips.

"Lunch?" Maya repeated causing me to check out the clock on the wall behind my desk.

"No way, is that the time already? Where the hell is the boss? I should call him, he could be ill or have had an accident." I panicked, grabbed the phone on my desk and hit the speed dial that had already been pre-programmed to my boss' mobile first, or cell as my directory had it listed as. Well, he was American I supposed as I heard the tone that seemed to ring forever before connecting to what I had anticipated being an answer phone.

"You've reached Denton Miller's den of debauchery and iniquity. Unfortunately Mr Miller is unable to come to the phone right now as he is busy between my thighs, can I take a message?" the voice asked, the voice of a woman I was fairly certain wouldn't belong to Mrs Miller, so who was she, with her soft and subtle American accent that sang with amusement?

"I erm, sorry, I'm, my name is P.A., well not, I, erm," I stammered while Maya watched on with a horrified expression that was in stark contrast to her grin. With a deep breath and a wipe of my free sweaty palm down my thigh I composed myself and tried again. "This is Eloise, Eloise Ross, Mr Miller's P.A. He was expected in his office this morning…" I allowed my voice to trail off so that my words might register when I heard another voice on the end of the line, a man's voice.

"Tia, what are you doing? How many times have I told you, do not answer my phone? That's not your place."

I glared down at the receiver in my hand wondering how my husband had got his views on my new boss so wrong. Arrogant prick I thought, except when I heard Tia giggle down the line and Maya stifle a laugh with a gulp, I realised that I had said it, out loud.

"It's your office, your P.A.," Tia explained. "Checking up on the boss."

This woman was also a pain in the arse, her and my new boss, maybe they were meant for each other.

"No, no," I stammered before I heard Mr Miller's reply.

"I don't need checking up on. I'm going in now, as per the email I sent to my P.A. Could this day get any worse?" he asked as I flushed crimson despite him being unable to see me.

"Did you get that, honey?" Tia asked still laughing.

"Yeah, got it, thank you, sorry, sorry to have interrupted your erm, sorry," I cried and hung up. "Oh bollocks, his day has nothing on mine!" I told Maya slumping into my chair.

"And you kind of hung up on him at the end there." She smiled with an accompanying cringe.

"Oh God! Why am I even doing this? He was so sweet on webcam," I said, thinking aloud.

"With Mr Stanton?"

I buried my face in my hands. "Shit, yeah. He was with a woman, maybe not his wife and like with her with her I think." My whispered realisation made Maya laugh loudly.

"So, to sum up, you have inarticulately interrupted a secret shag, somehow made it sound like he was a naughty boy by being late and then hung up on him?"

My horrified expression must have conveyed how awful I felt because Maya appeared before me on her haunches.

"It wasn't that bad babe. He'll be fine, I'm sure. Come on, lunch." Getting to her feet she pulled me to mine. "Come on, no arguments, we'll go to the pub over the road, no alcohol, just food."

Nodding, I grabbed my things and then quickly checked my emails, only to find an earlier email from my boss.

Morning Ms Ross,

I was hoping to be in before you this morning, but I had to change plans.

Will be very late afternoon so may not get to meet you until tomorrow as I have a busy day planned.

Regards,

Denton Miller
CEO Miller Industries (Europe)

"Oh," I whispered almost undetected as a second email hit my inbox.

Ms Ross,

Thank you for the nurse maid duties, however

208

unnecessary they were. I am able to tell the time and arrive at the office without assistance!

After further changes to my first day I may not make it into the office at all today.

I shall expect to see you in the morning no later than 8 a.m.

Oh, and Ms Ross, don't ever fucking hang up on me!

Denton Miller
CEO Miller Industries (Europe)

"He's really got to be kidding me, hasn't he?" I asked pulling Maya to see my second email, but she literally just squealed with some kind of delight.

"I think I am going to enjoy working here, a boss that emails with swearing and a bollocking! Come on, lunch, I only have cover on reception for one hour, meaning we now have exactly forty seven minutes to be back here."

Every mouthful of my linguini that tasted like shoe laces rather than pasta got stuck where I imagined my gullet might be, even with the assistance of two glasses of a non-alcoholic beverage.

"Do you think he'll sack me?" I asked Maya who had no problems digesting her food that was a steak and ale pie with seasonal vegetables and seriously chunky chips.

"No, I wouldn't have thought the interruption of a mid coital rendezvous with his mistress would be classed as a sackable offence."

"Thanks," I replied, wondering what else I could say to that and decided there was no more to say.

I returned to my office, which was actually a working space within Mr Miller's office space. I suppose it could be seen that I occupied his vestibule or an atrium, the space between his inner sanctum and the world beyond, although as this space happened to be at the furthest point of the building everywhere else was the world beyond. I liked that a small amount of reworking had been done up here so I didn't mistake the office as Michael's, it was Mr Miller's and I couldn't, wouldn't forget my place. As well as my work space, this area also housed his reception area, the place where I'd be responsible for entertaining any visitors who were waiting for my boss. Maybe if he was finishing off Tia, or whoever.

With I sigh I observed the boxes of stationery that still littered my floor and decided to tackle them, get to the bottom of it all, just not yet. After a cup of coffee, if I could find where the coffee machine was housed. Yes, that was a plan. Coffee, and just in case my wayward boss turned up I'd take my photocopying down the hall with me and make myself look busy.

It was another forty-five minutes before I found myself back at my desk, with coffee and the photocopied proposals that Mr Miller would need later in the week. The mess on my floor was worse than I had remembered. Could this day get any worse I wondered once more as another email hit my inbox?

Ms Ross,

You appear to have littered the floor with semi-unpacked boxes of stationery, please resolve this issue. Also, why do we have such a ridiculous amount of compliment slips and headed paper? We live in an age of electronic communication. I think you may have overstocked somewhat. Again, resolve before tomorrow morning.

I am out for the day. In the event of an emergency, I repeat, EMERGENCY you may call me!

I take my tea with just a dash of milk, no sugar, and coffee no milk, one sugar. I drink tea until 10 a.m. and coffee thereafter, unless I instruct you otherwise.

Regards,

Denton Miller
CEO Miller Industries (Europe)

"Fucking numb nuts," I told him even though I was alone. The cheek of this man. "I have semi-unpacked the stationery that was ordered by someone else, not me, and I know we live in an age of electronic communications, so I have not overstocked anything and yet I am expected to sort it. I will call you when hell freezes over after my initial attempt at contact and on top of that I am now your tea girl!"

The sound of my phone's ring brought me back to the here and now, Michael.

"Hi, you okay?" I answered.

"Yes, just checking in. How's your day going?" he asked and as much as I wanted to vent I knew he wouldn't get it. He'd turn everything on its head and blame me. Not me personally, but my position, so I replied accordingly.

"The new boss had a change of plan. He appears to have popped in, a visit I missed and now he's not in until tomorrow, but things are fine."

"You don't sound sure? Maybe you should think about scaling back, love."

Oh my God! I actually wanted to scream at him because he was the retired one, not me, I wasn't even half way there. Why the hell would I want to scale back, but as usual he continued to speak.

"There's a group, at the hospital, a support group for families. You could help them out, or Johnny at the golf club was saying they're looking to take on a part timer to help with memberships..."

I cut him off, abruptly. "Michael, I don't want to scale back, nor work at the golf club, nor listen to people discuss how hard it is to, well, whatever. Denton Miller may prove to be more of a challenge than I had first imagined, but it's fine. What do you fancy doing this evening?" I asked hoping he'd say something exciting, different to the norm, maybe even dinner, alcohol, a bath and an early night.

"I'm easy, whatever you want darling, although there is a

documentary on the demise of the bee on at half-past eight so I'd like to be done by then."

"And an early night?" I suggested, hating myself a little for pleading for his time, attention and his penis. This day really was turning to shit.

"El, I don't know, we'll see," he said, the dismissal obvious in his tone.

"I might be going out straight from work," I lied. "Maya is back here, she's the exec's receptionist now, so I thought we might catch up, in the pub, or a bar or something."

I was slightly disgusted with myself for lying so blatantly to my husband. Something I'd never done, about plans that didn't exist, but the mere thought of sitting and listening to a blow by blow account of why bees were disappearing made me want to cry. Almost as much as the idea of drinking cocoa before finding myself sitting up in bed reading stories of passion and romance while my husband slept next to me, snoring, having managed to fall asleep in the time it took me to wash my face and brush my teeth.

"Oh, okay, well let me know when you've decided what you're doing, and remember me to Maya."

"Okay," I whispered before guiltily but honestly adding, "I love you, Michael."

"I know darling, and I love you too."

Throwing my phone into my bag I felt shittier than I might have ever felt, but more than that I felt discontent, sad and restless, and possibly a little reckless.

Printed in Great Britain
by Amazon

41680391R00121